Also by
Carlton Mellick III

WHY I MARRIED A CLOWN GIRL FROM THE DIMENSION OF DEATH

CARLTON MELLICK III

ERASERHEAD PRESS
PORTLAND, OREGON

ERASERHEAD PRESS
P.O. BOX 10065
PORTLAND, OR 97296

WWW.ERASERHEADPRESS.COM

ISBN: 978-1-62105-358-3

AUTHOR'S NOTE

Have you ever seen clown porn from the early 2000s? If you haven't, please don't. That shit was fucked up. I still have nightmares about it.

—Carlton Mellick III 7/16/2023 2:19pm

CHAPTER ONE

Clowns creep me right the fuck out. They always have, ever since I was a little kid. Those shrill laughs and misshapen features, the crazy style of makeup and hair, the wicked smiles on their faces, everything about them has always made my skin crawl. I've jumped out of airplanes, slept with spiders, and was even buried alive during a college prank, but I don't think there's anything more terrifying on this green Earth than coming face to face with a clown.

My clown phobia has always been a problem for me, but it got a whole lot worse a few years ago once gateways to other dimensions started popping up all over the city. Beings from other worlds have been migrating here and becoming a part of our culture. There are cat people from a dimension where humans evolved from felines instead of apes. There are robot people who come from a reality where people transcended their human flesh and turned themselves into machines. And there's even a group of giant cockroaches who are more intelligent than the most brilliant minds in human history. But the species that bothers me the most is the race of clowns that emerged from dimension 162, most commonly known as the dimension of death.

It's called the dimension of death because it's considered by far the most dangerous of all the dimensions discovered in the last few years. It is full of giant predatory insect-like creatures that would decimate the population of our planet if even one was able to fit through the gateway. The world has rivers of acid and lakes of fire and oceans of flesh-eating bacteria. It is described as a dimension of Hell on Earth. And on top of all that, it has clowns. Billions upon billions of clowns who are making their way through the dimensional portals into our world.

The clowns from the dimension of death are not like the ones from our universe. They aren't just normal people wearing makeup and floppy shoes. They are born that way. They are horrific feral creatures that live in alleyways and lurk in the shadows, giggling like madmen and feeding on human souls.

Ever since the clowns came into our world, I've been terrified to leave my house on the off chance I might run into one. I haven't been able to go to work or shop for food. All I do every day is search the internet to read horror stories of clown sightings and conspiracy sites talking about how the clowns are responsible for all the children who have gone missing on the news. I know all of these stories are from less than reputable sources and have been created just to get a rise out of people like me, but I can't help but believe them. Deep down I see clowns as nothing but vile, evil creatures and I don't see how my opinion of them will ever change.

But I know I can't let fear run my life. I know I have to get over it. If I get fired and lose my house then I'll be out in the streets and probably surrounded by clowns that populate the homeless camps on the outskirts of the city. My boss said that he would keep me on disability as long as I start going to therapy, so that's what I plan to do. I doubt I'll be able to get over my phobia but I'm hoping it will at least give me the strength to leave the house and go to my job. I don't know what else to do. I could move back in with my parents but the clowns have been migrating to cities all across the planet. There's no way to escape them. I just have to learn how to deal with them if I ever hope to get my life back in order.

"When do you think your fear of clowns began?" the therapist asks me.

I sat down not five minutes ago and she's already getting right to it. It's not the first time I've been to a therapist. I suffered from depression and social anxiety when I was in college and my parents sent me to a psychologist so that I'd stop skipping class and they wouldn't waste all the money they put up to send me there. But that psychologist took things slowly. It was several sessions before he finally asked me why I was depressed, telling me to focus more on exercise and giving up caffeine before he'd even hear out my problems. But this lady doesn't mess around. She has so many patients since the gateways opened up that she probably doesn't have the time to beat around the bush. A lot of people's phobias have probably escalated in recent years. Not just because of how rapidly our world is changing, but because people are struggling with religious beliefs and fears of strange alien life forms entering society. There aren't just clown people, but spider people and snake people and rat people and all manner of horrifying races. Therapists are in more demand than ever.

"Since I was five years old," I tell her, sitting awkwardly in the tacky brown suede armchair across from her. "The first time my parents took me to a circus."

The therapist maintains eye contact with me as she adjusts her glasses and brushes her long dirty blond hair from her shoulders. A clipboard rests in her lap but she doesn't appear to be interested in writing anything down. She just wants to hear me out.

"What happened that was so frightening to you?" she asks.

"Well, I'd never seen a clown before, not even in pictures. I didn't know what the hell the thing was. I saw it as some pot-bellied monster that grabbed me and picked me up in its horrifying arms, laughing as I thought it was trying to kidnap me."

The woman nods. "And what did your parents do?"

"They thought it was hilarious. They just laughed at me as I cried and told the thing to hold me up so they could take a picture. The clown said he liked me so much he wanted to take me home with him and my parents jokingly told him that he could. I was convinced I'd never leave the circus ever again."

"It sounds like that would be upsetting to any five-year-old."

I shake my head. "But that was just the start of it. After my parents realized I was terrified of clowns, they spent the next few years of my life tormenting me about it. They thought it was funny to hang up posters of clowns in my closet or play circus music from an old cassette player in the attic. One time my dad even dressed up like a clown on Halloween and stood outside my bedroom window calling out my name."

The therapist bursts into laughter and holds her hands in front of her mouth. It's the same response I get whenever I've told anybody about my childhood experience and it pisses me off more than anything.

"Do you think it's funny?" I ask in an annoyed tone.

The therapist shakes her head. "I'm sorry… I think it's a little bit funny."

"It's not funny," I say, raising my voice. "It was child abuse. Whenever I was bad, they threatened to take me to the circus and leave me there. They told me I'd stay with the clowns forever."

The therapist holds back another laugh. "But your parents loved you, didn't they?"

I nod my head. "Yeah, but they were still assholes."

"Did you ever think that maybe they were doing it to help you get over your phobia? Making light of what we fear is a good first step in overcoming this kind of thing."

"But what they did was what created my phobia.

They terrorized me for their own amusement."

"Well, parents are human, too. They don't always make the best decisions." She looks at her phone to check a recent text. "Were they young at the time?"

I nod my head. "They had me when they were teenagers. My dad was still in college at the time."

"And how old are you compared to the age they were?" she asks while scrolling through her messages.

"Right now? I'm probably ten years older than my dad was."

"Do you think you would have been a perfect father when you were his age?"

I shrug. "I wouldn't have tortured my child like they did."

"How is your relationship with your parents now?" she asks, half-focused on reading a message on her phone.

"It's fine, I guess. They live in Colorado so I only see them whenever they can afford to fly me out for Christmas."

"Do they still play practical jokes on you?"

I shrug. "Not since I was a kid, about the time they gave up drinking."

"Were they heavy drinkers?"

"Not really. Occasionally, when tequila was involved. They mostly drank on weekends, after I went to sleep."

The therapist puts her phone down and returns eye contact. "So what other experiences with clowns have you had since you were a child? Anything as traumatic as when you were five years old?"

I shake my head. "Not really. I couldn't watch movies

with clowns in them. I've never been to a circus since then and divert my eyes whenever I see clowns in public. I just avoid them as much as possible. It would be fine if it weren't for the nightmares."

"Nightmares?"

"I dream about clowns from time to time. Horrible dreams. They're worse than anything that happened to me in the real world."

"Care to tell me about them?"

I shrug. "Not really. They're just nightmares."

"I'd like to hear about them."

"Well, think of a zombie apocalypse but with clowns instead of zombies. I'm usually alone in a deserted city filled with deranged clown-like creatures that hunt me for food."

She smiles. "Yeah, I'm sure that would be scary. Do you ever have problems sleeping? Do you stay up late in order to avoid your dreams?"

I shake my head. "They're not that common. I only have them a few times a month. But when they happen, they really freak me out. I'm usually full of anxiety for days after."

"What about after the 162 gateway opened?" she asks.

I take a deep breath. I fold my hands in my lap to keep them from shaking. "That's where the real problems started. My dreams stopped being so scary once the clowns from my nightmares came into the real world."

"Do you think the clowns from 162 are the same as the clowns from your nightmares?"

I just nod my head.

She says, "You described the clowns in your dreams as zombie-like monsters that eat human flesh. Do you really think the people from 162 are like that?"

"Not exactly the same, but... kind of. I've read all about them on the internet."

"Have you ever met one in person? Have you ever spoken to one face to face?"

I shake my head.

"If you ever sit down and talk with one of them you'll see they're just normal people like you and I. They aren't anything to be afraid of. They aren't monsters."

"They're monsters to me."

The therapist takes a deep breath and sighs. "We live in different times now, Timothy. You have to understand that your views are now considered racist by a lot of people. Now that they're a real race of people, being afraid of clowns is no longer acceptable. Imagine if you came into my office with a fear of homeless people and insisted they were monsters. Do you really think that would be okay?"

"But I'm not afraid of homeless people. I have a cousin who is homeless."

"And would you want anyone to see him as a monster?"

"No, of course not. But that's different. He's not a clown. He didn't come from another dimension."

"But the clowns live here now and they're here to stay whether you like it or not. You might have to live next door to one someday. You might have to work with them. You might have a daughter who marries one. You might have half-clown grandchildren."

The thought of having clown grandchildren sends a shiver down my spine.

"If you can get over your phobia it will be what's best for you and everyone around you. If you let your fear control you then you won't be able to see clowns as human beings. If you are in a position to hire employees for your company you won't be able to stop yourself from discriminating against clowns. You'll blame clowns for everything bad that happens in your community. Prejudice against anyone, even clowns, is a terrible thing."

I look down at my hands. It's the first time I ever thought of myself as a racist before. Clowns weren't a race when I developed my phobia, so I never thought of my fear as a prejudice. It kind of makes me feel like a piece of shit. But just because my fear is filling me with guilt doesn't mean the fear isn't real. It isn't just going to go away.

"I want you to meet someone," the therapist tells me. "There's a clown who recently moved into my apartment building who said she's interested in meeting new people. She wants to make a friend. She's a very sweet girl, about your age. I think you'll like her."

Her words alarm me. I'm shocked she would even suggest such a thing.

"Wait a minute," I tell her, holding up my hands. "I'm not cool with that at all."

"I just want you to meet her. It doesn't have to be for long. I think if you spoke to someone from dimension 162, even for a little while, you'd understand how normal they are. You'd be able to see them as human beings instead of monsters. It's the best way to overcome your phobia. If you want to return to work or ever lead a normal life, this is the only way."

"But isn't it too soon? I'm not ready."

"It's best to drop you right into the deep end and see how well you swim. If you can't handle it then I'll know right away and have her leave the room. But I need you to try."

I shake my head. "I don't think I can…"

"I'll be there with you," she says. "She'll come to your next session and we'll just a have normal chat. It will be completely safe."

I feel myself beginning to perspire. Sweat is forming on my brow. My heart is pounding in my chest. I just want to refuse and go home and find a different therapist, one who isn't going to make my phobia worse. But I know that could get me fired. If my employer learns I couldn't last more than one session, I'll surely be out of work. I don't think I have a choice.

"Do I have to do it sober?" I ask her.

She looks at me with a smirk. "What do you mean?"

"Can I have some drinks beforehand?" I ask. "Back when I suffered from social phobia in college, I used to be fine if I drank alcohol while spending time with other people. It'll make it easier."

"That's usually not something I'd agree to," she tells me. "Using alcohol to fight a phobia will only lead to other problems."

"I don't think I can do it otherwise."

The woman sighs and pauses for a moment, staring at

me. Then she says, "Okay, the first time you meet with a clown you can drink. But only a couple drinks. And if it goes well, I'd like you to do it again when you're sober."

I nod my head. "That's fine." But I know for a fact that it's not going to go well enough for a second try.

"Instead of meeting at our office, how about we meet at a bar? Let's not treat it like a therapy session. We'll just be three friends going out for drinks after work."

"I can do that."

"Great," she says, standing up to see me out. "Then I'll talk to Puppy and set up a date."

"Puppy?"

"That's her name. Puppy Caterpillars. It's a clown name."

She sees me out of the room and says her goodbyes. Then calls in her next patient from the crowd of terrified people who are also struggling with the beings from other dimensions that populate our city. There are dozens of them, even more frightened than I am. It makes sense the therapist would be pushing me to get over my phobia as soon as possible. She doesn't have time to mess around. Hopefully, she knows what she's doing. If her methods make me worse than I already am I'll probably have to move into my parents' basement and lock myself from the world and never go out in public ever again.

CHAPTER
TWO

I meet the therapist at an upscale cocktail bar near her office. It's not my scene, the kind of place twenty-somethings with a lot of disposable income go after their high-paying tech jobs to drink kimchi bloody marys and gummy bear martinis while bitching about white privilege on social media using MacBooks that cost more than my car. But since the therapist is charging it all to the account that my employer is paying for, I don't have to worry about the prices. I order the strongest drink on the menu, some kind of tropical rum drink with a little umbrella that the therapist doesn't realize is basically just a tall glass of Bacardi 151.

I'm two-thirds into the drink with a good buzz going by the time the clown arrives.

"There she is," the therapist says, pointing at a woman on the far side of the room.

I glance over at the clown for just a second and then look away. Just the sight of her bright blue polka-dot dress is enough to put me into a state of shock. I down the rest of my drink and tell the waitress to get me another.

No matter how much alcohol is in my system, I'm just not ready for this.

The therapist calls out to the clown and invites her to the table. I don't look up from my empty glass as she sits down on the stool across from me. As she greets the therapist, I can't help but cringe at the sound of her voice. She speaks with a strong accent, but it's not any accent I've ever heard before. A clown accent. It's a little high-pitched and squeaky like her voice is filtered through a dog toy. She sounds like a cartoon character. Because the clowns speak their own language, she isn't completely fluent in English yet. It makes her sound kind of like a baby.

The therapist introduces me. "This is Timothy, the guy I told you about."

A paper-white hand with bright blue fingernails reaches its way across the table. When I look up, I find myself face-to-face with the clown girl. Her eyes are massive, almost taking up her whole face. Huge purple eyes staring at me with a big smile on her blue lips.

"Hi, I'm Puppy!" the girl says with childish excitement.

I can't look away from her. She's not as clownish as I expected. She doesn't have as many colors as clowns usually have. She has short blue hair and pink triangles around her eyes. A pink nose and long tentacle-like eyelashes that flash at me in a way that sends shivers up my spine. But she's not as scary as I was expecting her to be. She's very petite, barely five feet tall. Slender and delicate. Even if she was a monster she wouldn't be able to cause me harm if she tried. She's still frightening with her pale white skin and cartoon-like features but she's far less threatening than I expected her to be.

Before I realize what I'm doing, I reach out my hand and let her shake it. Her skin is smooth and soft, but room-temperature. It's like clowns aren't as warm-blooded as humans are.

It might be because of the alcohol, but without thinking I say, "I like your fingernails."

The clown girl releases my hand from her grip and holds up her nails. "I know! Aren't they pretty? I was blessed with blue fingernails even though my mom's were orange and my dad's were purple."

When she says this, it creeps me out a little. I thought I was complimenting her choice of nail polish without thinking that she was born that way, that her fingernails were naturally blue. For some reason, that distinction makes them less attractive than I originally thought.

The therapist sees the awkward look on my face and steps in. "Timothy here has never met anyone from dimension 162 so he's excited to talk to you."

Her words leave me stunned and I stare at her in disbelief. She knows full well that I was dreading this meet-up and want nothing to do with anyone from the dimension of death. But as I scowl at her, the therapist just winks at me. The clown girl lights up with happiness when she hears about this.

"Oh wow!" Puppy says, gazing intently at me with her large purple eyes. "I've been excited to meet people from your world as well. I've been here for over two years and it's been so hard to make a friend. So many people seem scared of clowns. I'm so happy you're not one of them."

After I hear this, I get annoyed at my therapist. I'm sure she never told the girl that I'm terrified of clowns. I wonder if Puppy even knows why she's meeting with me. It makes this so much harder if she doesn't know I'm meeting with her for therapy.

When my second drink arrives, I grab it from the waitress and down half the glass in a single sip. The clown girl orders the fruitiest tropical drink on the menu and looks back at me.

"I'm fascinated by the people of your world," she says. "You have so many wonderful things that I didn't have in my dimension. I love your movies more than anything. We didn't have television sets where I'm from. Nor the internet or music videos or comic books. It's so amazing."

The therapist interjects. "Puppy wants to be an actress. She loves creative types like you."

"Yeah!" Puppy cries. "I've been wanting to make friends with people in the creative industry. You're an artist, right?"

I shake my head. "I just do digital art for an advertising firm."

Puppy gives me a confused look and turned to my therapist. "What's that?"

The therapist explains, "He does the art in the commercials that you see on television."

When she hears this, her eyes light up. "Oh wow! I love commercials. They're like tiny movies."

I shake my head. "It's not a big deal. I just do whatever art they tell me to do. It's not a glamorous job."

Puppy doesn't acknowledge my words. "I'm trying to get roles acting in commercials. Maybe we'll work together someday."

When Puppy's drink arrives, I can't believe the sight of it. The thing was designed specifically for a clown. It has blue and pink stripes of fruity alcohol with whipping cream and cotton candy on top. The curly straw even has a little teddy bear on it, holding balloons and sparklers.

Puppy takes a big sip of the drink and looks up at me with whipping cream all over her face. As she wipes it away and licks her fingers, I realize I'm not as frightened of this woman as I thought I would be. She's definitely strange. She's definitely creepy. I don't see her as human at all. But she's more like a cartoon character than a monster. If all clowns are like her, I might actually be able to deal with them in our world.

My therapist sees me relaxing a little and then looks at the time on her phone. She says, "I should be heading out now. I've got another appointment at four."

When she says this, my eyes light up in shock. "Already?"

Puppy frowns at her. "But I only just got my drink."

"You two should stay," the therapist says. "Enjoy yourselves. I've got work to do."

I look at the woman in disgust. She knows full well I'm not comfortable with her abandoning me. She said she'd stay the whole hour but it's barely been ten minutes since the clown arrived.

"Well, as long as I can keep drinking with Timothy,

it's okay if you go," the clown girl says. She flashes her weird tentacle eyelashes at me while sipping on her straw.

Before the therapist leaves, she walks to me and whispers in my ear, "You'll be fine. If you can't handle it just tell her you have to go to the bathroom and sneak out."

I give her a dirty look. "But that would be rude."

She shrugs. "Then don't do it. I'll see you at your next appointment."

The therapist waves goodbye to Puppy and pays our tab. Then she leaves me alone with the clown girl, the same creature that's given me horrific nightmares for my entire life.

I was just starting to feel comfortable around a clown for the first time in my life, but now that I'm alone with her I can't help but let my fear take over. My hands are shaking, my heart is pounding. I have no idea what to say. I just want to scream and run out the door.

As her big glossy eyes scan me over, she recognizes how frightened I am. It makes her smile.

"You look nervous," she says. "Have you ever been on a date with a clown before?"

Her words bother me. Does she think we're on a date just because we're alone now? I'm only doing this for therapy. I have no desire to get to know her outside of that.

I chug the rest of my drink and shake my head. "I've never even spoken to anyone from your dimension before."

She raises her eyebrows. She doesn't exactly have eyebrows, but she raises the marshmallow-white flesh on her brow and says, "So I'm your first? That makes me happy."

She smiles.

"Why does it make you happy?"

"Because clowns are territorial," she says. "They don't like sharing friendship with each other. If you made friends with another clown they would get upset with me having drinks with you."

I have no idea what she's talking about, but I let it slide.

"Has it been hard adjusting to life in a new world?" I ask her.

She gets happy that I asked her a question. She probably would have reacted the same no matter what I asked her.

"Not at all! Where I come from, things were so much different. People don't have it as easy as we do in your world. Survival is not something we take for granted."

"Everyone calls the world you come from the dimension of death," I say. "Is it really as dangerous as people say?"

She laughs. "Compared to this world, yes. But I didn't know how bad we had it until I came here. People in your world have it so good. You're able to enjoy your life in a way that my people never could."

"Why do you say that?"

"Life is so fleeting in my dimension. People die all the time, so easily. We try to spend every minute of every day living our life to the fullest. We try to entertain each

27

other, and make each other laugh, to get our minds off of the death that surrounds us at all times. We never imagined what it would be like to live in a world as safe as this one. Clowns living here can put all of their energy into being happy and entertaining each other. It's completely changed my outlook on life."

"Is that why you want to be an actress?" I ask.

She smiles. "Yeah! I can be an entertainer here without worrying about whether I'll still be alive tomorrow. I can plan for the future. It's such a different way of life than I'm used to."

After she says this, I start to realize how important it was for my therapist to introduce me to this woman. It's really changing my opinion of clown people. I was always scared of the clowns who came from the dimension of death, but I never thought about how difficult it must have been to live in such a dangerous world.

"Do you ever plan to go back?" I ask.

"Hell no," she says. "No, no. Never. There's nothing in that world that I'd trade for living here."

"Not even your family?"

"It's hard to keep track of family there. Once you get separated from people, you rarely find them again. Even your parents or children. You just stick with whoever you can for the sake of survival. It doesn't matter if you're family or strangers. Sometimes it's easier to leave family behind so that you don't have to see them die."

"Did you ever see members of your family die?"

She nods her head energetically, as though the thought doesn't bother her at all. "I've seen loads of them die in all kinds of horrible ways. But I was too busy laughing and running away to be disturbed by their fate."

"Laughing?"

"Yeah, clowns are taught to laugh when faced with death. We all want to die laughing. It's so we can enjoy every last second of life we have left before we meet our gruesome end."

"I assume the life expectancy in your world isn't very high."

She nods. "We typically don't live past thirty. The oldest clown I've ever met was thirty-eight."

"So there are no old people where you're from?"

She shakes her head. "The concept of old people was new to me when I came to your world. I had no idea that people get wrinkled and frail if they live too long. I'm excited to see what it'll be like to actually grow old here."

When the waitress comes back, Puppy orders us another round without consulting me about whether I want to keep drinking with her. I figured two drinks would be plenty and I could go home happy that I succeeded in holding an actual conversation with a clown, even without the therapist. But Puppy isn't letting me go of me that easily. I'll have to spend at least one more drink with her. But I have to admit that it's not been unpleasant talking to her. She's more like a normal person than I expected she would be. And learning about her world and old way of life is quite fascinating. I wouldn't mind hearing more about it.

After three more drinks, I'm feeling pretty sloshed. Puppy tells me crazy stories of giant creatures from her world and how she survived several encounters with them. She tells me about the walled circus-like towns that once existed long before she was born and how most of their technological advancements only happened during this small era of their history. When I ask why the clowns from her world look so much like the clowns from ours, she doesn't have an answer for me. She tells me that clowns evolved to have brightly colored skin to scare away predators, warning them that they might be poisonous.

"But are you poisonous?" I ask her.

She happily nods her head. "Yeah, actually we are in a way. Clowns excrete a paralyzing toxin in our sweat. When a predator eats one of us, it will become immobilized for a short time, long enough for the rest of us to escape. But it only affects the smallest of predators. It does nothing to ward off the bigger, more dangerous ones."

"So the clowns from your world have nothing to do with ours?"

She shrugs. "I don't know. They sure look a lot like us. It's almost like they were based on the people from my dimension."

"Perhaps the dimensional gateways opened up for a short time in human history. Maybe my ancestors met one of yours in the past and based the style on them."

Puppy nods with excitement. "Yeah, maybe that's true! There are stories of vanilla clowns that resembled humans like you in our world a long time ago."

"What happened to them?"

Puppy shrugs. "I don't know. They died out I guess. Or they just mated with clowns and all of their descendants would no longer be recognized as human anymore. Some people say that I am a descendant of vanilla clowns since I'm not as colorful as the majority of my people."

I nod my head at her words. If that's true, if Puppy really is a descendant of my world, maybe that's why I'm not quite as frightened of her as I am normal clowns. She might be a rare exception. But if humans went to the dimension of death and clowns came to our world, what happened to the clowns that settled here? There are no descendants of clowns in our history. Unless they were all hunted down and exterminated as demonic beings from hell, which is very possible. A thousand years ago, clowns would not have stood a chance.

We change the subject and focus more on movies and comedians Puppy likes and all the things that she enjoys about living in a new world. After a while, I realize everyone in the bar is staring at us. It might be because of how loud we've become from drinking so much. But it seems more likely that people are staring at us because they are weirded out by the fact that a human is on a date with a clown. I'm not actually on a date with her, but I'm sure that's how other people see it. The feeling of their eyes on us makes me uncomfortable.

There's one guy who bothers me in particular. He's sitting at the table next to us, drinking by himself and typing on his phone like he's frantically shitposting on

Twitter for no reason whatsoever. The guy is a semi-short zillennial with scrubby facial hair, bushy eyebrows, and thick black-rimmed glasses. He looks up at us and then down at his phone, as though we're the ones he's talking about on the internet. When Puppy isn't looking, he stealthily takes a picture of us and goes back to his phone. The guy is really beginning to piss me off. I wonder what his problem is.

When he catches me glancing over at him, he gets out of his seat and approaches us with an annoyed look on his face. But I'm not the one he speaks to. He goes up to Puppy and gets in her face.

"I find that offensive," he tells her.

Puppy has no idea what's going on when the guy confronts her. Her eyes widen and flinches back, terrified of being yelled at by a random stranger.

"What do you mean?" Puppy cries, clearly upset by his words. "Did I do something wrong?"

The guy rolls his eyes. "Seriously? Do I have to spell it out?"

She points at me in a panic. "I'm just sitting here with my friend. I don't even know who you are."

He takes another picture of her on his phone.

"What's your name? I'm posting this on social media."

"I'm Puppy. Why are you posting about me on social media?"

He rolls his eyes again. "Because you're wearing clownface. Don't you know how offensive that is to real clowns?"

Puppy looks at me with a confused expression and

then back at the hipster. "What's clownface?"

"It's when people dress up like clowns. That's not cool anymore. It's racist."

Puppy's mouth drops open. "But I am a real clown."

The hipster just types on his phone, ignoring her words as though he's positive she's lying to him.

"I come from dimension 162," she tells him. "I'm not wearing makeup. I'm not wearing a wig."

She grabs his hand from his phone and puts it in her hair. The guy's eyes light up in a panic once he realizes that he's been mistaken. He completely changes his tune.

"Oh my god, I'm so sorry," he cries. "I didn't know."

He keeps apologizing and begging for forgiveness, as though he's worried *he's* going to be the one to be canceled if anyone ever finds out that he made such a mistake.

"You look so normal, I thought for sure you were a human in clownface," he says.

"Normal?" I ask him.

He ignores me, turning his back to me so he can block me out of the conversation. "That's so cool you're a real clown. I've always wanted to meet one."

"Really?" Puppy says. "Not a lot of guys are interested in meeting clowns like me."

The guy speaks in a flirtatious tone when he tells her, "I'm not like other guys."

When I realize the hipster is hitting on Puppy in front of me, it makes me feel jealous for some reason. I have no idea why, since I'm not the least bit interested in the clown girl, but the guy is seriously getting on my nerves.

"I'm actually a content creator who fights against

clown prejudice," he says. "I think it's really unfair how your people are portrayed in media these days. I'm doing everything in my power to bring attention to the mistreatment of clown immigrants in our society."

"Umm... okay," Puppy says. "I didn't know that was a thing."

"It is," he says. Then he digs a business card out of his wallet. "I'd like to interview you on my podcast. I have over five thousand followers. It would be great if I could get your story out to the people."

After he says this, I can't help myself anymore. He has to be one of the biggest douchebags I've ever seen. Obviously, he's just trying to fuck her and doesn't care about what she's really going through since she moved to our world. If she actually is facing prejudice in our world it's probably nothing compared to what she had to deal with when she lived in the dimension of death. The guy doesn't understand her at all. He probably just has a clown fetish.

"Excuse me, we're kind of having a conversation here," I tell him.

The guy puts his card down on the table in front of Puppy and then turns to me. He glares at me with a challenging look on his face.

"And what have you done for clown rights?" he asks me. "Do you think just dating a clown makes you an ally?"

"We're not dating," I say. "We just met."

"Guys like you disgust me," he says, getting in my face. "You don't realize how oppressive your behavior is by dating someone from a position of power."

"I already said we're not dating," I argue.

I now realize the guy is incredibly intoxicated, even more so than I am. He's slurring his speech and being overly aggressive, obviously just envious that I'm drinking with a clown girl when he's not. He has no idea I'm just trying to get over a phobia.

"You probably want to turn this girl into your play thing," he says. Then he takes another picture of me. "You're so going on Twitter."

He types on his phone violently, like he's participating in a fight with me but taking it online instead of swinging his fists. Before he can click send, Puppy grabs his phone from his hand and drops it in her drink.

The hipster freaks out. "What are you doing? I'm trying to help you!" Then he turns to me. "This is your fault!"

As the hipster tries to dig his phone out of her glass, Puppy jumps to her feet and grabs me by the arm. "Let's go."

She tugs on my wrist, pulling me to my feet with strength that shouldn't come from a woman of her size.

"But we haven't paid our bill," I say.

"Forget about it," she tells me, taking me out of the bar and running down the street, laughing at the top of her lungs in a high squeaky pitch.

The hipster yells out of the bar at us. "Fuck you, brainwashed bitch!"

But we keep on running, down the street and out of sight, laughing at the creepy entitled podcaster who continues to spit obscenities in our direction.

With adrenalin running through my system, the alcohol hits me way harder than it was back at the bar. Everything is spinning and I can't walk straight. But I feel better than I have in years. The liquor puts me in a dumb state of bliss that makes me happy just to be alive. When I look over at Puppy, I see her smiling at me. I'm not sure when it happened, but she has my arm curled around hers, pressing herself tightly against me as we walk down the sidewalk. She stares deeply into me with her big eyes.

I stop in my tracks and look closely at her. The irises of her eyes are transforming from purple to a dark blood red.

"Your eyes…" I say. "They're turning red."

She smiles at me in an almost frightening way and says, "Clown eyes change color based on our mood. Mine are usually pink but become purple when I'm excited and brown when I'm sad."

The idea of mood ring eyes both fascinates and worries me. I start to remember she's not a human or from my world. She's an alien creature and nothing like any woman I've ever met before.

"What does red mean?" I ask. The blood-red color is worrisome, like she's ready to kill someone. I wonder if the guy at the bar pissed her off and made her angry.

But Puppy doesn't look angry. Her smile is almost seductive. She has a thirsty look in her big glossy eyes.

She leans in closer to me and says, "It means I'm sexually aroused."

Then she pulls me into an alley and pushes me against a wall and kisses me deeply. At first, I'm shocked and want to shove her away from me, but the alcohol in my system dulls my fear and I find myself kissing her back. I wrap my hands around her and let her kiss my face and neck with her slimy blue lips. My mind fades and I just go with it. I close my eyes and let all of my fears and nightmares fall right out of my head.

CHAPTER
THREE

I wake up the next morning with the clown girl in my bed with me. Her long slender feet hang out the bottom of the covers like seal flippers, exposing jagged blue toenails that haven't been cut in months. Her white arms wrapped around me, holding me as tight to her as she possibly can, smiling in a deep sleep.

I barely remember how we got here, just hazy scenes of us going back to my place and tearing each other's clothes off. I don't remember having sex with her. I pray we didn't have sex at all. Maybe we just made out a little and passed out in my bed naked. But when I look under the covers, I see my penis is coated in a sticky paste covered in glitter. I have no idea what it is until I scrape some off and smell it. The glittery goo is definitely some kind of clown vaginal fluid. We definitely had sex last night.

"What the fuck?" I cry, rubbing the glittery fluid against my bed sheet.

All at once, a surge of fear rushes over me and I'm gripped by a paralyzing terror toward the woman in my bed. She holds my body so tightly to hers that I can't escape. Her horrifically colored face presses against my shoulder, snoring in an unnerving squeaky tone. I have no idea what to do, so I just lie here for an hour, waiting for her to wake up. Paranoid about what will happen when she regains consciousness. I never should have drank so much. I was so proud of myself for being able to hold a conversation with a clown for so long. I should have let it end there. This is probably the biggest mistake I possibly could have made and will likely become only more afraid of clowns than ever before.

When Puppy finally opens her eyes, she's not as shocked as I was when I woke up. She stretches and yawns, then smiles up at me and pulls me closer to her like a teddy bear. It doesn't seem like she was too intoxicated last night. It's like she knew exactly what she was doing and has no regrets.

She laughs as she squeezes me and says, "I'm so happy! I finally made a human friend." Then she tucks her head into my armpit, her blue hair covering my naked chest. "You're my friend now, right?"

I don't know how to answer the question. I wish I had an excuse to leave the bed and get away from her, but because it's my home and I don't have work to go to there's nothing I can say in order to escape.

I find myself saying, "Yeah, sure."

She giggles and puts her marshmallow-white hand on my chest, rubbing her blue fingernails into my skin.

"That's so wonderful," she says. "I was worried that you just cared about sex and didn't want to be my friend."

After she says this, I wonder if there's a translation

issue with what she's saying. I don't know if she means what I think she means.

"By friend, what exactly are you talking about?" I ask.

She lifts her head and looks at me with swirling reddish-purple eyes. "You know. You're my boyfriend and I'm your girlfriend. That makes us friends."

My eyes widen when she says this. "Wait, do you think being friends means we're in a romantic relationship?"

She snickers. "Yeah, of course. What else would it mean?"

"We call acquaintances friends. It doesn't mean that we're romantically involved. Being boyfriend and girlfriend is a different thing."

She's confused by this. "I don't understand. Isn't friend the gender-neutral way of saying girlfriend and boyfriend? I assumed it could mean either one and is inclusive to people who are nonbinary. I thought using inclusive terms was a big part of human culture."

"Well, it is, but we don't call someone we're romantically involved with a *friend*."

"Then what do you call a boyfriend or girlfriend who isn't a boy or a girl? Wouldn't they just be your *friend*."

"I don't know."

She lifts herself up and looks down at me, exposing her naked body. Her nipples are dark blue and there is a flower-shaped spiral of pink around her breasts. The sight of them surprises me. I had no idea clowns had such colorful markings on their bodies below their faces.

"So what kind of friends are we?" she asks with a concerned face, her eyes turning orange.

I don't know how to respond. "I'm not sure. We're the normal kind of friends."

She still seems upset and confused.

"So are you my boyfriend now or not?"

Her question scares me. I don't want to be her boyfriend, but I don't want to make her angry, either. I have no idea what will happen if I make her angry.

Uncertain of how to reply, I find myself saying, "Yeah, I'm your boyfriend."

Joy radiates across her face and she lunges at me, pressing her naked body against mine and holding me close. I have no idea what I've just done, but there's no way to take back what I've said. My heart is pounding in my chest. There's no way I can really date a clown.

But as she holds me, I feel a sensation of calm. Something vibrating through her soft lukewarm skin puts my mind at ease. It's almost like she's purring against me, releasing euphoric chemicals into my skin. I've been lonely for a long time and haven't been in a relationship with a woman for years. I wonder if I *can* date Puppy. Maybe being with her won't be so bad. Maybe it will get me over my phobia for good and make my life happy and fulfilling.

But once Puppy goes home, telling me she'll stop by later that night, I find myself in a state of complete dread. I take a shower and wash the clown pheromones from my skin, feeling sick to my stomach and barely able to keep myself upright. I have no idea what I'm going to do.

When I go to the therapist's office for my next session, I can barely contain my nerves. I'm even more freaked out than I was before.

"What happened to you?" she asks, holding back a snicker.

I shake my head. "You have no idea."

The therapist points at my face. "What are those things on you?"

She's talking about the blue kiss marks on my cheeks and neck. If I took my shirt off she would discover my entire body is covered in them.

"Puppy made them," I say. "She kissed me all over and left them on my skin."

She smiles. "So things went better than I expected the other night?"

I just look away from her, not ready to talk about it.

"Why didn't you wash them off?" she asks.

I look back at her and say, "They don't come off."

"What do you mean?"

"Her lip prints are permanently embedded into my skin. She said they'll never come off for the rest of my life. Like tattoos."

"How is that possible?"

I shake my head. "It's a clown thing. When clowns choose lovers, they leave kiss marks all over their bodies to scare off other women. It's a way of claiming a mate as her property. Other clown women won't go anywhere near me as long as I have these on my skin. It releases a smell that will be unpleasant to any other clowns but Puppy."

The therapist moves in closer. "Yeah, you do smell pretty bad. Kind of like a dead skunk."

"You smell it, too?" I cry. "I thought only clowns were able to smell it."

The therapist shakes her head. "I guess it works with all members of the opposite sex."

Mind reeling, I ask, "Did you know about this?"

She shakes her head. "It's the first I've heard about it. I've never seen kiss marks on male clowns before."

"So I'm going to be stuck with these for the rest of my life? Are all women going to be repulsed by me?"

The therapist shrugs. "Tattoos can be removed. Perhaps there's a way to laser them off."

When she says this, I'm able to relax a little. At least there's still hope. It will be expensive but at least I won't be stuck like this forever. I would be so pissed if Puppy made me completely repulsive to all women but her.

"So tell me what happened after I left the other day," says the therapist. "I take it you spent quite a while together."

My face turns red. "I got way too drunk and we ended up in bed together."

"That's a pretty huge step to take for someone who's afraid of clowns."

"It's your fault it happened," I say.

"How is it my fault? You could have left the bar at any time."

"Puppy was under the impression that you were setting

us up on a date. When she told you she was looking to make human friends, she meant she was looking for a human boyfriend."

"How was I supposed to know that?"

"You shouldn't have left me alone with her. I was too drunk to know what I was doing."

"You wanted to be intoxicated when you met her. If you had limited yourself to two drinks like I recommended, then you wouldn't have made a decision you now regret."

I look away, knowing she's right. I understand it's immature to blame her for my own poor judgment, but I wanted to be mad at someone and she seemed like the right person to take out my frustration on.

The therapist changes the direction of the conversation. "So are you planning on seeing her again?"

I sit there quietly for a moment and then say, "Yeah, we're dating now. We've been seeing each other every day since the last session."

The therapist's eyes light up. "Are you serious? How has it been going?"

I shrug. "I'm not comfortable with it. It's hard getting over the fact that she's a clown. If she was a normal girl, I'd be beyond happy with her, but she's so... alien. Otherworldly."

"Well, she is literally from another world. Of course she's going to be otherworldly."

"But I never thought I'd fall in love with someone so creepy to me."

"So you've fallen in love with her?"

When I realize the words I used, my eyes widen and

then I shake off the thought.

"I don't know…" I say. "I barely know her."

"But you think it's possible you could fall in love with her?"

I just shrug. "I don't know… Maybe."

"What have you been doing together since you've been dating?" the therapist asks.

"Mostly we've been watching movies at my place. She wants to watch every single movie I like, so we've been going through my old Blu-ray collection. *Corpse Bride* and *The Dark Crystal* are the two she likes best. She didn't like *Raging Bull* or *The Godfather* trilogy."

"Have you been intimate with her?"

The question throws me off. I feel awkward admitting it, but decide to tell the truth.

"Yeah, pretty much every time she comes over. She can be very aggressive."

"Is it consensual? If you're not ready for that level of intimacy you should be honest with her about it."

I shrug. "It's mostly consensual, I guess."

"Mostly?"

"Well, clowns sweat a paralytic poison. Sometimes when she's making out with me I absorb too much of the poison and lose the ability to move. Whenever this happens, she always takes advantage of it and I can't do anything to stop her. I probably wouldn't resist her if I wasn't paralyzed, but I don't like feeling that helpless around her. I can't even close my eyes when she stares at me with her creepy face."

"That doesn't sound like a healthy relationship," the

therapist says. "You should tell her not to do anything to you whenever you're paralyzed."

I just shrug. "I don't want to be paralyzed at all."

The therapist nods her head and changes the subject, "Are you using protection?"

She's beginning to sound like my mother.

"No, whenever we have sex I'm usually not in the right state of mind to make good decisions."

The therapist nods and looks at me with a concerned expression. "You should be aware most people from other dimensions have no concept of birth control, especially not the people from dimension 162. They come from worlds more dangerous than ours, where breeding often is important to their survival. They view sex as a way to increase their numbers. Puppy lives in our world now, but she still has the instincts of someone who was born in the dimension of death. Whether she knows it or not, she could be acting on those instincts. Now that she's in a safe place, her body could be telling her it's the perfect time to breed. She might not even know why she's so driven to have sex with someone she barely knows. They don't see relationships the same as we do. They probably don't even have a concept of marriage or monogamy. Sex is for making babies. You might be getting yourself into something you're not ready for."

When the therapist finishes, I can't even speak. My heart sinks into my chest and I fill with panic. I knew having unprotected sex was a problem, but I was just worried about getting some kind of weird clown STD. I wasn't thinking I might get Puppy pregnant. I guess I just assumed she was using birth control.

"You should make sure to have a long conversation with her about this," says the therapist. "Make sure you wear a condom if you don't want her to get pregnant."

I'm full of terror when I ask, "What if she's already pregnant?"

The therapist shrugs. "You're an adult. You should've been aware of that possibility."

"But I don't want to have to marry her. I don't want clown children."

She shakes her head. "That's your prejudice coming through again. It's incredibly racist to say you don't want *clown* children."

"I don't care if it's racist," I tell her. "I don't want clown children!"

The therapist lets out a sigh. "Well, just talk to her about it and tell her how you feel. Let her know you don't want children yet. As I said, clowns don't see relationships the same way we do. Even if she gets pregnant, she might not want to get married. She might not need you to be a father."

I put my elbows on my knees and rub my face in my hands. I feel like such an idiot.

The therapist says, "All that aside, I feel like you're making incredible progress. You've been able to spend this much time with a clown and haven't regressed at all as far as I can tell. How are your dreams? Are you still having nightmares about clowns?"

I shake my head. "Not really. I have dreams where Puppy crawls into my bed at night and makes love to me, but that's usually because she is doing it for real. I've woken up twice to discover her in bed with me, even though I went to sleep alone and locked the doors and windows. I'm not sure how she's getting in."

"You need to create boundaries. Tell her how inappropriate that is."

I shake my head. "I don't want to make her mad."

"Why not?"

"I'm afraid of what will happen if I get on her bad side."

"Do you think that's healthy?"

I shrug.

"If you don't want her breaking into your home at night you need to let her know. She's not going to get mad. She just doesn't clearly understand human etiquette, so of course she'll make mistakes. She probably doesn't have any malicious intent."

After she says that, I mostly remain quiet until we run out of time and the therapist sends me home. The words *malicious intent* are stuck in my mind. I feel like that's my problem. I can't shake the feeling that everything Puppy does has malicious intent. But I think it's my phobia, my own prejudice, making me feel that way. There's nothing evil about Puppy. I'm just having a hard time letting go of my fears. I need to get over myself. I need to try to see Puppy for who she is. She's not just a clown. She's not the same as the monsters of my childhood.

CHAPTER
FOUR

For the next few weeks, Puppy and I see each other more and more frequently. I try telling her about the boundaries my therapist said I should make with her, but she doesn't seem to listen too much. She always changes the subject on me and talks about whatever random thing she's excited about that day. I said she can't break into my room at night, but she still shows up whenever she wants. She got a key to my front door made without me knowing, so now she can let herself in without having to crawl in through a window, as though the problem was the method she used to get in rather than that she was coming over unannounced.

I try wearing condoms whenever we have sex, but Puppy never lets me keep them on for long. She pulls them off of me in excitement whenever she sees them, then blows them up like balloons and bounces them in the air. I'm not sure if she does it because she really likes balloons or because she is trying to get pregnant, but I haven't been able to convince her of their importance one bit.

Every time she shows up at my house, she brings more

of her stuff with her, slowly taking one bag of belongings at a time until she's fully moved in. She doesn't ask me if it's okay that she lives with me, but she hasn't left for the past few days and I'm beginning to think she's here to stay. My house is now full of clown things. Balloons and unicycles and fluffy pink teddy bears bigger than she is litter my house. My therapist says that I need to talk to her about it, but I can't get myself to stand up to her. Puppy is so happy every single minute that I spend with her that I can't handle the thought of making her sad. She might be taking advantage of my timidness or she just doesn't see anything wrong with what she's doing. Either way, I'm letting her get away with whatever she wants even if it's to my own detriment.

And when she brings up the topic of marriage, she catches me at a time when I'm at my most weak and vulnerable. She's standing naked in front of me, a few minutes after we had sex. A bottle of whiskey in one hand, a bottle of whipping cream in the other. Her dark blue pubic hair is itchy against my lower abdomen when she sits on my lap.

She wraps her hands around my shoulders, staring into me with deep red eyes. Her thick blue armpit hair drips with poisonous sweat.

"So should we?" she asks in a thick clown accent. Her accent is always stronger whenever she drinks. "People are so happy when they get married in the movies."

I don't know how to respond to her proposal. It was so casual and sudden.

"But we haven't even been together for a month," I say.

52

"I don't care," she says. "I don't want to be with anyone else."

"You don't want to be with another clown?" I ask.

She sticks out her tongue with disgust. "Ever since I came to this world I only wanted to be with a human. Clowns don't love each other that way. They don't dedicate themselves to one person like humans do. I want romance, like in the movies. Clowns don't understand romance."

"But relationships aren't the same as they are in the movies. Those are fiction. They're fantasy. Real relationships are hard work."

Puppy seems confused. She surely knows the difference between fantasy and reality but doesn't understand the concept of embellishing stories to make them more entertaining to watch.

"But I don't want a fictional relationship," she says. "I want a real one. I'm willing to do whatever it takes to make it work."

"What if we grow to hate each other?"

"How could that happen?" she asks. "We're perfect for each other."

"How are we perfect for each other? I don't even know what you see in me."

She thinks about it for a second. "Well, you're human."

I laugh at her response, realizing how offensive that would have come across if someone from our world said that to someone they liked.

"But there are billions of humans in this world," I tell her.

"Yeah, but you don't run away screaming when you

see me like other humans," she says. "You're not afraid of clowns."

I laugh again. If only she knew just how afraid of clowns I actually am. I have to fight the urge to run away screaming every time I see her.

"Is that all?"

"No," she says. "There are hundreds of things I like about you."

"Like what?"

"We fit together right," she says. "Like peanut butter and jelly beans."

"Don't you mean peanut butter and honey?"

She shakes her head. "No, better than that."

At first, I think it's weird that she thinks peanut butter and jelly beans go together, but then I think about it for a second. Our relationship really is like peanut butter and jelly beans. She's the repulsively sweet jelly beans and I'm the bland salty peanut butter. If she thinks those two things go together it would make sense that she'd think we go well together, too. But I don't have the same tastes as she does.

"Our dreams are also aligned," she says. "You work in the movies and I plan to be an actress."

I shake my head. "I'm not in the film industry. I work for an advertising agency."

She shrugs. "Same thing. Commercials are movies, too."

"We mostly do magazine ads," I say.

She brushes off my words and says, "In my world, women choose men who make them feel safe and happy.

And I've never felt safer or happier than when I'm with you."

"How do I make you feel safe? I'm not a strong man. I'm far weaker than you are. I'm not athletic. I wouldn't be able to protect you."

"But I've never been in danger whenever I'm with you. It doesn't matter how athletic or strong you are. Clowns value luck and cunning more than strength, because the predators in my world are far more powerful than even the strongest man. Your luck is incredibly attractive to clown women."

"How am I lucky? I never thought of myself as lucky."

"Well, you have a big safe house. You have tons of food. You can spend hours and hours with me and we never get attacked by predators."

I laugh. "I'm only lucky because I was born in a world without the same dangers as yours."

"It doesn't matter. The fact that you have the life you do makes you more attractive than every single man I've ever known from my world."

I don't know what to say to her. She pretty much described the majority of men in the country. It's like she's only interested in me because I own a house and have a decent-paying job. I'm not unique in that way.

She looks at me with her big purple eyes and says, "Besides, you're really cute. You have a big movie collection and your penis is hard whenever you see me."

I'm disturbed by that last part until I realize I have an erection. She grabs me with her soft white hands and squeezes. Then she explains how clown men all have a difficult time getting erections. Because they are in a constant state of danger, always afraid of being attacked, it's difficult for them to get aroused. Their anxiety keeps the blood pumping to other parts of their bodies. Sex doesn't come as easily to them as it does in our world.

But the thought that I get an erection whenever I see Puppy is surprising to me. I didn't realize my body was reacting to her in that way. What is it about her that I find so arousing? It wasn't like this with girls I've been with in the past. I'm normally not having erections so frequently, especially not right after we already had sex. I'm terrified of clowns. I'm not turned on by them. I have no idea why my body is reacting to her in this way. Perhaps it's because I haven't been with another woman in a long time. Or maybe, like her, my instincts are taking over and urging me to mate. It's so frustrating to have my own biology betray me in this way but I can't help myself.

She lifts a floppy clown foot from the ground and presses it into my lap, curling her marshmallowy toes around my penis. As she strokes me, she stares deep into my eyes. Her irises turn a blood red color and then she lifts herself up to put me inside of her.

As she fucks me, squeaking and moaning in my face, she says, "So will you marry me?"

I find myself responding with, "Yeeeah."

But I'm not responding to her question. I'm responding to the feeling of being inside of her.

Her face lights up. "You will? You'll be my husband?"

I don't know how to take it back. I can't just change

my mind and tell her no. I know I need to say something, but I can't get over how good it feels to be with her in this moment.

Before I know what I'm doing, I tell her, "Yes, I'll marry you. I'll marry you so hard."

Then she laughs out loud in excitement and fucks the hell out of me right there on my living room couch. When we're finished, she wraps herself around me and kisses more blue lip marks all over my chest, giggling with glee, holding me like I've agreed to become her personal property.

Once my erection is gone and my sexual desires fade, I wonder what the hell I just did to myself. This has to be the worst thing I've ever done in my life. But, as she holds me tighter, filling me with euphoric chemicals, purring against my body, I start to wonder if maybe it will be a good thing to marry this woman. Nobody has ever cared for me like she does, not even my own parents. Maybe she really is the right person, even if she is a clown. Besides, the kiss marks on my body are never going away. I am now completely repulsive to all other women. It might be a good idea to at least give the relationship a try. I might never be able to find love with anyone else ever again. It would be a horrible mistake to give this up just because of my stupid clown phobia. I'd hate to live the rest of my life regretting what might have been.

I don't tell any of my friends or family that I'm engaged to a clown. I can't handle what they'd say about it. Not because I'm worried they might have a prejudice against clowns, but because they all know about my clown phobia and will likely make fun of me for it. I haven't spoken to any of my friends since they got married and started families, and my parents live across the country, so it won't be difficult to hide it from others for as long as I need to. If they find out they'll think I'm crazy or assume my phobia has somehow turned into an unhealthy fetish. The only person I plan to tell is my therapist since she introduced us and will likely be happy for me. If not because I've found love but because it will show her I'm recovering from my fear of clowns. I might even be able to go back to work soon.

But when I meet the therapist for our next session, she has a look of terror in her eyes.

"Are you still seeing that clown girl?" she asks me, panic in her voice.

"Yeah," I respond.

She doesn't give me time to explain more about how our relationship has evolved and says, "You have to get away from her."

"What are you talking about?" I ask.

She comes to me and sits in the seat next to mine. "I'm so sorry I didn't believe you. I thought your phobia was just paranoia. But you were right. The clowns are monsters."

Her words have me concerned. "I don't understand."

"I ran into a clown last night. Some large man with big red shoes and a bald white head. I saw him murder someone. I'm pretty sure it was a child."

She's trembling and ready to burst into tears. She speaks with such distress, I can barely follow her when she says, "I was walking home and saw it happen in an alleyway I was passing. The clown unhinged his jaws and swallowed the kid whole. At least I think it was a kid. I only saw two little legs dangling out of his mouth just before he gulped them down his throat."

I shake my head. "How is that even possible? Are you sure you weren't imagining it?"

"Hell no," she says. "I definitely saw what I saw. That thing's stomach was swollen to three times the size of any stomach I've ever seen. Then he turned to me and just giggled like a madman. He held his belly and laughed, jiggling the person inside of him. It was so disgusting. I ran away and locked myself in my apartment. I've been terrified ever since."

I don't know what to think of her story. If this was three weeks ago, I would have believed her outright. I definitely used to think clowns were capable of doing something like that. But now that I know Puppy, I think it can't possibly be true. I know that clowns are not the horrific monsters I used to think they were. The therapist must be testing me. She's probably checking to see how I'll react to hearing such an outlandish story. Somebody with a clown phobia would believe it immediately. Somebody who sees clowns as normal people wouldn't be so gullible.

"I'm sorry, but I don't believe you," I tell her.

She shakes her head, really putting effort into her performance. "No, it's true. I thought if anyone would believe me, it would be you. This is serious. These clowns are monsters invading our world. We have to do something about it."

I'm surprised she's taking the act so far. She must realize I'm not falling for it by now.

"Have you noticed anything weird about Puppy?" she asks. "You've spent a lot of time with her. Has she done anything weird? Has she ever tried to swallow a child?"

I almost laugh at her words. I couldn't imagine Puppy doing anything so horrible.

I say, "No, of course not. She wouldn't hurt a fly."

The therapist shakes her head. "That's just an act. She has to be a monster just like the one I saw. Get away from her as soon as you can. She's dangerous."

"But we've moved in together," I tell her. "We decided to get engaged this week. I plan to marry her."

The therapist's eyes widen in horror. "You have to call it off! She's not what you think. She's a clown from the dimension of death. Everything from that world is evil."

When she says this, I begin to think maybe she's not putting on an act. She seems to be serious. She's not testing me. She really did see a clown eat someone.

"The clowns are invading our world and coming to get us!" she cries, suddenly becoming even more deranged than before. She grabs me by the arm. "You need to run away from her. Run as far as you can! The clowns aren't humans. They are going to kill us all!"

She squeezes my arm so tightly that I cry out in pain. I pull myself from her grasp and get to my feet. "What the hell's wrong with you?"

As I back away toward the exit, the deranged therapist reaches out to me with tears flowing down her cheeks. "I'm sorry I didn't believe you. You were right all along. The clowns are coming to get us. We need to stop them. We have to do something before it's too late!"

I rush to the door and run away, leaving her in her frantic state. I can hear her screaming and crying from her office, yelling at me like an insane person. All of her other patients are alarmed, terrified by the woman's outburst. She is supposed to be their therapist. She is supposed to be the sane one, helping them with their paranoid delusions. But she's coming across as the craziest of the bunch.

A few days later, I learn that she's been put on leave indefinitely. Instead of going to see a different therapist, I decide to go back to work. The therapist's words didn't increase my fear of clowns. In fact, they seemed to have cured me completely. Seeing the woman in such a deranged state made me think of how I used to be. It made me realize just how silly I've been all these years. She probably mistook what she saw in the alleyway. There's no way a clown was eating a child. I've been with Puppy for weeks and there's never been any kind of sign that she could physically be capable of doing such a thing. The whole idea is absurd.

I move on with my life as a new person, one who is not controlled by fear. I have a great life ahead of me with Puppy. She's unlike anyone I've ever known. She's a kind and beautiful person. One crazy woman's fears aren't going to stop me from being happy.

CHAPTER
FIVE

Puppy and I get married. We decide against a big wedding and just elope so that we can call each other husband and wife as soon as possible. I still haven't told my parents about it and probably won't until I see them next Christmas. For now, I just want to be with Puppy as much as possible. My clown phobia has completely disappeared. I don't see Puppy as anything but the love of my life. She's so weird and adorable, eating candy for breakfast and leaving balloon animals for me in bed every time I wake up in the morning. Even her high-pitched squeaky laugh is growing on me. Instead of being creepy, I see it as incredibly cute. She has turned my life upside-down and I'm so thankful for it. I've never been happier.

But it doesn't take long before I notice some things that are *off* about my wife. Things I didn't realize until after we got married. For instance, I never got a good look at her teeth before. Clown teeth are much different from human teeth. They are more like the teeth of sharks. I notice it the first time we eat red meat together. I make us a rack of lamb with mint jelly. When she picks up the large piece of meat, she opens up her mouth so wide that I see what is hidden within. She has rows of sharp teeth, hundreds of them. They tear into the flesh and pulverize the meat behind her wet blue lips.

As she chews, I stare at her in horror. She just stares back at me and smiles, holding out her hand to grab mine, and says, "It's *so* good!"

Just like sharks, she loses her teeth frequently. While eating the lamb, she pulls out three of them and leaves them on the table next to her plate. She discards them like nothing, like losing teeth is the most normal thing in the world to her.

For the next few days, I find her teeth scattered across the house like fingernail clippings. They get stuck in the shower drain and in the garbage disposal. They are hidden in the carpet and stab into my heels whenever I walk barefoot through the house. I've had to pull four of her teeth out of my skin so far and every time they leave horrible wounds that become itchy and infected almost instantly.

The idea that clowns have teeth like those of sharks would have been terrifying to me before I met Puppy, but they are more of an annoyance than a threat. Still, it is alarming that clowns have such different anatomy from humans. Her teeth only become a real concern whenever she wants to give me a blowjob. I can't possibly refuse her when she offers to give me oral sex, but the experience is far too unsettling to be pleasurable. When my penis is in her mouth, all I can think about is how easily it would be to tear my member apart. My penis wouldn't stand a chance against all those pointed teeth. I could be emasculated in an instant, even by accident, and there's nothing I could do to stop it.

But the shark teeth are not the only alarming part of being married to a clown. In the late spring, clowns spin webs like spiders. Silky wires come from a gland above Puppy's rectum. She strips down naked and climbs up the walls and across the ceiling, building intricate webs across our living room. Then she props herself in the center of the web, awaiting prey to get stuck within the sticky fibers.

When I ask what kind of prey she's trying to capture, she tells me, "Step in the web and find out."

I humor her by walking into her web and find myself stuck, completely unable to move. The sticky strands are stronger than steel, binding me to the spot. I try pulling away, but my arms won't budge. I'm completely trapped.

"Okay, let me go," I tell her. "This isn't funny."

She glares at me with blood-red eyes and crawls down her web toward me. "Why would I let my prey escape? I caught you fair and square."

She curls me up in her web and makes love to me, sucking on my neck like she's trying to drain me of blood.

Besides making webs in the living room, she puts a lot of effort into building them in the backyard. She creates a whole labyrinth of spider webs that make it difficult for me to get fruit from my plum trees or cook steaks on the grill outside.

One day, Puppy catches a neighborhood dog in her web. The little terrier dug its way into our backyard and found itself trapped in the silky strands. When I come outside to see what all the whimpering is about, I catch Puppy attacking the helpless animal. She opens up her jaws and bites into the creature with three rows of shark teeth, tearing flesh from its tiny body, eating it alive as it cries and struggles.

It's the most horrible thing I've ever seen. When the dog is half-consumed, I approach Puppy and ask, "What the hell are you doing?"

She just smiles at me and says, "I caught some lunch. Do you want some?"

"That's the neighbor's dog!" I cry. "How could you eat it?"

She shrugs and takes another bite, peeling off its hide in her teeth and chewing on it like a gory fruit roll-up.

"It's sho good," she says with her mouth full.

Puppy doesn't understand the difference between food animals and pets. In her world, there probably wasn't a concept of pets. She probably ate any meat she could get her hands on, no matter how cute the animal was. But we have plenty of food in the house. I don't know why she felt the need to kill something for food. When she's done, I have to bury the remains in the yard, hoping the old lady next door never finds out.

But it's not the first animal Puppy catches in her webs. She preys on squirrels and birds, rats and snakes. Eating them with her horrific jagged teeth, her eyes rolling into the back of their sockets, tearing flesh from bone and chewing it like a wild animal. Even though clowns were hunted by giant predators in their dimension, I'm learning they were far from the bottom of the food chain. They, too, are fearsome predators in their own way. Puppy is proving to be less and less a civilized being the more I spend time with her.

No matter how many animals she eats alive or how many webs she builds around the house, my fear of clowns does not come back until I learn about a strange behavior Puppy exhibits between 2 a.m. and 3 a.m. every night. I'm not sure if this is normal behavior for Puppy or normal behavior for other clowns. I'm not sure if it's something Puppy has been doing ever since I've known her or if it's something completely new. But for one hour a day, every day, Puppy becomes somebody else. Not the woman I married. Not the sweet person I fell in love with. She becomes a strange feral creature.

I call it *clown hour*. For one hour a night, Puppy loses herself. Her eyes bulge out of their sockets. Her irises and pupils shrink to tiny black dots that terrify me whenever she looks in my direction. Her lips stretch into a wide horrifying smile that takes up her entire face, exposing her jagged shark teeth. Then she runs through the house, her arms twisted and malformed, creeping through the

67

unlit hallways like some kind of hideous creature.

Whenever I catch her in this state, her head will spin around, making a bone-cracking noise. Then she'll crawl up onto the ceiling and chase after me, crab-walking backward with her head on the wrong way, giggling like an insane person. If I can't escape in time, she'll drop down on top of me. Her head will crack back into position and she'll make love to me right there on the floor, glaring at me with her zombie-like eyes, giggling like something from my nightmares.

I'll tell her all about it when she wakes up the next day, but she has no idea what I'm talking about. It's like it never happened. She thinks I'm making a joke. But it's really happening. Every single night. If I'm asleep she'll usually just leave me alone during clown hour, but I find it difficult to sleep knowing it's coming. I try hiding under the covers, pretending to be asleep whenever I feel her get out from under the covers and twist her limbs into knots around the room. But she often will climb up onto the ceiling and look down at me, just staring and drooling at me like I'm a small animal she's caught in her web.

Puppy sweats a lot during clown hour, making it very easy to paralyze me whenever she catches me. But she never hurts me once I'm in her grasp. She either makes love to me or just holds me down and stares into my eyes with her horrible zombie-like gaze. I begin to wonder if Puppy is acting completely on instinct during clown hour. Maybe she is driven by hunger and desire. It's not uncommon for her to raid the refrigerator during this time, devouring all the raw meat we have planned for meals that week.

But it's not just Puppy that's affected. It's common for me to see other clowns running through the neighborhood past 2 a.m. on occasion. I'll see them through the windows, running down the road with their heads twisted back to their spines, laughing and squealing, chasing after neighborhood cats.

There have been several reports on the news about clown attacks that happen during this time. The clown conspiracy sites have been going crazy, saying there's a secret war that clowns are waging against humanity. That the clown apocalypse is approaching. I begin to wonder if the clown my therapist said she ran into was during clown hour. Perhaps what she said was true, but it was during a time that the clown was not in his right senses. Maybe if she saw him at another time she might have seen him as a normal person instead of a monster.

I should be even more terrified of clown hour than I am, but knowing that Puppy always turns back to normal at three in the morning makes me feel safe. She's still the woman I fell in love with. She's still Puppy. As long as she's not violent during these episodes, I think I can get over it.

Even as I wake up in the middle of the night to find Puppy unhinging her jaw and trying to swallow me alive, pulling my feet through her mouth and down her throat, I don't panic. I'm too big for her to swallow. She gets me up to my thighs and then spits me out the second I struggle against her. I look at her with an annoyed face, more upset that she woke me up than that she tried to eat me. But she just laughs and crawls up on top of me and shoves her long clown tongue through my lips and down my throat.

She tries to swallow me a few times over the next month, but it never goes anywhere. It's gotten to the point where I just kick her away and roll over and go back to sleep. I've realized the secret to dealing with clown hour is to have sex with Puppy before bed every night and make sure she gets plenty to eat for dinner. If she gets both of those then I don't have anything to worry about. She just wanders the house for an hour and then goes back to sleep. And the next day I get my beautiful Puppy back.

CHAPTER
SIX

Puppy is pregnant. I'm not really surprised when it happens. We've been having sex nonstop since we first met. It was only a matter of time before it happened. I'm not ready to be a father, but the concept of having a child with Puppy is strangely exciting to me. Before, I would have been disgusted by the idea of having half-clown babies, but I have a completely different opinion of that now. The fact that I'll have a clown son or a clown daughter doesn't matter to me. I only care that it's a child made from Puppy and I. We'll have a child we can raise together, one that we can love and raise and bring into our lives.

It takes quite a long time for Puppy to realize she's pregnant. Even as her belly swells out, she doesn't notice anything different about her appearance. I try to explain to her that she has to be with child, but she just thinks she's been eating too much. It isn't until she swells up to the size of a beach ball that she finally accepts the fact. And once she comes face to face with reality, she couldn't be happier.

"We're going to have babies!" she cries. "They are going to be the cutest babies ever!"

But the closer it comes to delivery date, the more panicked I become. I don't know if I'm ready to be a dad. We have plenty of space for a child. I make plenty of money for the three of us. But when I think about clown hour, I wonder if a child will be safe in our house. What will Puppy do to the child when she's not in her right senses? Will she still keep it safe? And will our child be like Puppy? Will the child also go through clown hour every night? Do I have to deal with more than one crazy person crawling on the ceiling in our home? The thought makes me worried about the future. I can barely sleep at night.

When Puppy is finally ready to give birth, I'm shocked by what happens. She doesn't give birth to a normal baby girl or boy. She lays eggs. Dozens of them. She lays them in the spider webs in the backyard. Large ostrich-sized eggs that are green and pink with purple stripes and polka dots. Like Easter eggs dangling by webs from tree to tree. They glow a radioactive light, pulsing and throbbing whenever we get too close.

"There's so many of them…" I tell Puppy after she lays the last one.

She wraps her arm around me and stares at her brood. "It's a good batch. I don't think I've ever seen anyone lay so many."

"But… there's so many…"

Puppy nods. "Survival is so difficult in my world that it's important to lay a lot of eggs. It's the only way to continue our species."

I just stand there with my mouth wide open. "But we're not in your world…"

Puppy smiles. "Yeah, I bet most of them will survive here. Usually, only a dozen are even able to hatch. And of those only a few make it to adulthood. But in this world, I bet every single one of them will live long, fruitful lives."

I fall to my knees. I had no idea clown physiology was so much different from mine. What are we going to do with so many babies? I don't have the space in my house for them. I don't have the money to support them. There have to be at least forty eggs hanging in my yard. We're screwed. We have no chance of raising them all.

"We did good," Puppy says, scratching my head with her blue fingernails. "We should celebrate."

I just shake my head. "What are we going to do?"

"Well, we have to protect the eggs," Puppy says. "When clowns give birth they spend a lot of time fighting off predators who want to eat them. But since there aren't any dangerous predators in this world, it shouldn't be too difficult. What animals will eat our eggs in this neighborhood? Raccoons maybe? We just need to watch for raccoons. If they don't get stuck in the webs, we'll have to fight them off."

At this point, I feel like raccoons would be a blessing. If they could eat all of the eggs but one I would be happy.

"Let's drink some tequila and have sex," Puppy says. "I want to celebrate."

"Sex?" I ask, shocked by her suggestion. "You just gave birth. Why do you want to have sex?"

"Clowns always want to have sex after they give birth. It's when we're most fertile. When you're in a safe enough place to give birth, you want to keep going and lay as many eggs as possible. You never know when you'll have another opportunity to multiply."

"But we're not in your world," I say. "This will be way more children than we'll ever need."

Puppy doesn't listen and pulls me back into the house, stripping off my clothes and dragging me into bed with her. Unlike before, when we used to have sex just for fun, I can tell she's now fucking me with a different intention in mind. She wants more babies and wants me to give them to her. The look in her eyes is different than any other time she's made love to me. Her irises turn steel gray, a color I've never seen before. Based on the calm smile on her face, I assume the emotion she's experiencing is the satisfaction of becoming a mother. It's a kind of happiness you get when you're able to have children without the worry they'll be eaten by predators. Either that or it's some kind of emotion human beings have never experienced before. The kind of emotion that you'd only understand if you were raised in the dimension of death.

Several of the eggs are broken when we wake up one morning. Colorful eggshells are scattered across the yard, lying in puddles of glowing green yolk. Tiny dead clown fetuses buzz with flies, lying on the lawn in piles like dirty laundry that fell off a clothesline. They don't look at all like human fetuses. They more resemble insect larvae with blue noses and purple polka-dotted skin.

I have a hard time thinking of them as dead babies. They're my children yet I don't really feel any kind of loss or sadness. I'm more disgusted by them than anything. Since there are still so many eggs left, I don't see it as that big of a deal.

But Puppy is furious. Her eyes turn a deep yellow, the color of anger, with black spirals around her pupils.

"What did this?" she cries. "There aren't any predators here. Our eggs should have been safe."

Based on all the yolk-covered rocks scattered across the yard, I can tell exactly what happened. I bend down and pick up a stone and examine it, thick glowing goo drips from its sides.

"It wasn't a predator that did this," I tell Puppy. "I think it was some neighborhood kids. They must have thrown these rocks over the fence from the alley."

Puppy looks at me in shock. "Why would anyone do something so horrible? I thought humans were nice."

"Not all humans."

"They're monsters!" Puppy cries. Her eyes spin in their sockets, the black spirals twisting in a hypnotic way. "Why are humans such monsters?"

I shake my head. "Kids are just like that."

Puppy goes to the fence and looks out into the alleyway. "I'm going to kill them! I'll kill them if they hurt my babies!"

I go to her and try to calm her down. "They probably didn't know what they were doing. Humans don't lay eggs like clowns do so they didn't realize there were babies in them. They were probably just scared. They probably thought they were some kind of odd alien eggs from another dimension. If they knew they were killing babies I'm sure they wouldn't have done it."

"But why would they just smash them?" Puppy cries. Her eyes turn from yellow to brown and she wraps her arms around me, crying against my shoulders. "Why didn't they just ask us what they were?"

I just hold her and try to comfort her. "Kids are dumb. They don't think before they act. I was the same way when I was that age. I used to shoot birds with a BB gun. Or take their eggs from nests and throw them at walls."

Puppy looks up at me with sad eyes and asks, "Why would you do something so horrible?"

I shrug. "I thought it was fun at the time. I was a stupid kid who didn't know any better. Once I was older, I realized what I was doing was wrong and stopped being so mean and destructive. I matured."

"I hate human children!" Puppy cries. "They need to all die."

I shake my head. "We just need to be more careful. The kids won't do it again if we tell them not to."

Puppy cries again and puts her face in my chest. She pulls a row of brightly colored handkerchiefs from her sleeve to wipe the tears away. Then we clean up the eggshells and bury the dead fetuses in the flower garden.

We go door to door and explain to the neighbors what happened to our babies. We tell them the neighborhood kids have been destroying our eggs and we'd appreciate it if they kept an eye out for us. The neighbors are shocked by what we told them, but not because kids were killing our babies. They are more shocked by the fact that clowns lay eggs. They are terrified to learn that a clown in their neighborhood is producing a brood of clown babies right near their home. I hoped that doing this would protect our eggs from vandalism, but it might have done the opposite. It might have gotten a lot of adults interested in smashing the eggs as well. Not for the fun of it, but because they don't want dozens of clowns hatching in their neighborhood.

Puppy doesn't let her guard down after that. She sleeps in the webs outside, keeping an eye out for anyone who might want to harm her babies. She won't leave her eggs alone for a second, so I have to do all the shopping and chores around the house. All Puppy does day in and day out is keep an eye on her brood, protecting them from harm.

The only time she leaves the nest is during clown hour. I'll go out into the backyard after two in the morning and won't find her anywhere in or out of the house. It's like she's out prowling the neighborhood, hunting for the children who smashed her eggs.

I've been able to convince Puppy that the children who did this were not evil and do not deserve punishment.

They just need to be educated and it will all be okay. But when Puppy is in her zombie-like state, she probably isn't thinking clearly. She's acting on instincts and her instincts are telling her to eliminate everything that might be a threat to her young.

Two middle school boys go missing in our neighborhood. Nobody knows what happened to them until their bodies are found with their throats ripped out, lying in an alley five blocks away from our house. The authorities say it was like they were torn apart by wild animals. But I'm sure it was Puppy who killed them. The kids probably came back to our house during clown hour and Puppy, not being in her right senses, must have chased them down the alleyway and mauled them to death. I can't imagine what it must have been like for the young boys, chased by a thing from my nightmares and ripped to pieces by shark-like teeth.

But Puppy has no recollection of doing anything to those kids. Despite finding blood on her clothes, she doesn't think anything of it. Now that the children are dead, Puppy is suddenly in a much better mood. She is happy again, feeling that her babies are safe even though she doesn't quite know why. She doesn't even feel the need to sleep in her nest anymore and has returned to our bed. She goes back to making love to me, trying to get pregnant again so she can birth even more eggs, trying to make up for the offspring she lost.

Even though Puppy doesn't know what she did, I am completely aware that I'm married to a murderer. Perhaps I'm the only one who knows. And it's eating me up inside that my wife could have done something so horrible, all to protect some eggs we don't have the resources to care for if they all happen to hatch. But Puppy is in such a good mood I can't get myself to tell her about the blood on her hands. I worry the police might come for us, that they might sentence my wife to death or just shoot her down like a rabid animal, but I try to ignore my fears. I want Puppy and I to have a happy life together. I don't know for sure that she was the one who killed them. I know she wouldn't do such a thing if she was in her right state of mind. So I decide to let it go. I try to pretend it never happened.

The eggs grow larger with each passing day. They go from the size of cantaloupes to the size of watermelons to the size of pumpkins to the size of wine barrels. When Puppy is ready to give birth again, she lays smaller eggs in her web beside the larger ones. This batch is twice the amount of the last one. There are so many eggs, so many spider webs, that I can no longer see most of my backyard anymore. It's just a messy mass of webs and glowing, pulsing orbs.

When the clowns finally hatch from their eggs, Puppy is over the moon with excitement. Her eyes are the brightest purple I've ever seen. The clowns break out of their eggs one at a time, poking at the shells with bird-like beaks. The first of them is a naked blue-haired woman with green circles on her cheeks. I'm shocked when I see her. The clown is already fully grown, an adult woman who is both taller and more shapely than her mother. I had no idea our children would be born fully developed like this. I always assumed we'd have clown babies and see them grow into adults. But I guess clowns don't have time to be children. Surviving in the dimension of death requires babies to be born ready to combat their harsh world the second they step out of their eggs.

Puppy goes to her firstborn daughter and embraces her. She licks the green yolk from her face, peels the beak off of her face to reveal light blue lips, and hugs her close.

"It's okay, my love," Puppy says, caressing her wet blue hair. "You're with your family now."

Puppy pulls up her shirt and lets the woman feed from her breast. It's shocking to me that an adult clown woman would need to breastfeed, but it seems to be at least one thing clowns have in common with humans. She only feeds the girl for a minute before releasing her. Neon pink strawberry milk drips from her nipple and down the woman's chin.

Then she goes to the next baby. She feeds a male with short brown hair and pink skin, a boy that looks far more like me than his mother. The babies are born so quickly, Puppy doesn't have enough time to feed all of them. Many of the clowns pull themselves out of their shells and run away. They crawl over the fence and escape, going out into the world on their own.

I quickly realize Puppy isn't breastfeeding the children to give them nourishment. It's so that she can imprint them, so that she can claim them as her children. The ones who drink the strawberry milk from Puppy's breast stay by her side. All of the others escape, leaving the nest to go out on their own. By the time all of the clowns hatch, only five of them stay behind to be with their parents. The others are on their own.

"Come meet your children," Puppy tells me, waving me over.

I go to her and the five children that have stayed behind. Three women and two men, standing there naked with glowing yolk dripping from their bodies. It's so weird to see them as fully grown adults. They all resemble myself and Puppy, but it's difficult to really see them as my children. They are less clown-like than Puppy. Their colors are faded and they seem much more human than clown in a lot of ways. One of them even has the same color of skin and hair as I do. The only thing that makes her like a clown is the pink dot on her nose and the thin blue lines above her eyes.

"This is your Papa," Puppy says.

Then they come toward me, crying, "Papa! Papa!"

They gather around me and reach out their hands, grabbing at me. I hesitate at first, frightened of the fact that they learned speech so quickly. But when they grab me and huddle around me, cuddling against me for warmth, I begin to feel their purrs.

"Papa! Papa!" they cry in my ears, hugging me so tightly I can't move.

I let go of my fears and accept their love. They sniff at me and lick my neck, memorizing my scent. Despite my fear, I find myself hugging them back. I rub the yolk from their heads, squeezing their shoulders tight to me. These clowns are my children. I can't help but love them, no matter how strange they are to me. Puppy joins us and we have a big family hug.

I look up at her and ask, "What about the others? They all ran away."

For some reason, I'm suddenly worried about my other children. Even though I couldn't possibly take care of them all, I still feel a protective urge coming out of me. I want them to join our family as well.

Puppy shakes her head. "They're just decoys."

I'm confused by her response. "Decoys?"

"The predators in my world come running whenever a batch of eggs hatch. The others are designed to keep them occupied, sacrificing themselves so the primary children can escape. They instinctively run away from the nest to lead predators away."

"But there aren't predators in this world," I say. "What will happen to them?"

"They'll be fine," Puppy says. "They'll find their own way to survive without us. We don't have to worry about them."

I nod my head and focus more on the children who stayed with us, holding them tightly. But after thinking about it for a moment, I realize that we've just released a pack of feral clowns into the world. The clowns from my nightmares are now out there, haunting the city. These clowns won't know about our world. They will be a danger to our society. It makes me wonder if the clown my therapist saw was one of these. Perhaps she ran into a feral clown who didn't know any better. It fills me with guilt knowing that I've contributed to the increased number of terrifying clown creatures that roam our cities.

Now that we have five more adult clowns in our family, they take turns watching the rest of the eggs in our backyard. The children make their own clothing out of webs and dyes, creating colorful suits and dresses even more elaborate than Puppy's. I assumed the outfits Puppy wore were ones she bought from a store. I'm surprised to find out that she made them herself out of the web fibers her body produces. It's beyond strange to me that clowns can do this. Humans wouldn't be able to make their own clothes so easily, especially soon after being born.

Since Puppy has others who can look over her eggs, she has more free time on her hands. She spends it with me, making love to me in order to make more babies. I try to ask her when enough will be enough, but clowns don't seem to understand the concept of holding back. Her instincts are telling her to just breed and breed some more, multiply their numbers to secure the survival of her species.

During clown hour, all six of the clowns in my house lose themselves to their instincts. Luckily, my children sleep outside so I don't have to deal with them when I sleep. But I hear them crawling on the roof at night. I hear them running through the streets giggling in the moonlight. They are probably terrifying to everyone in the neighborhood, making them feel like they're being invaded by monsters from another world. Dead bodies are found from time to time, but I pray my children aren't the ones responsible. I stop listening to the news so that I don't know for sure. I don't want to take responsibility for my part in these incidents. I don't want to believe my family is murdering humans in the middle of the night. It could just be the feral children that didn't stay behind, but that doesn't make it any better. They still came from me. I wish clowns didn't have so many babies. Everything would be fine if clowns gave birth like normal people.

When the next batch of eggs hatch, Puppy is able to keep seven of the children. And the batch after that she gets eleven. Our clown children build colorful tents all around our property, creating a whole village around our home that makes it difficult for me to get out when I have to go to work.

The first batch of children are incredibly intelligent. They learn a full vocabulary of English within just a few months, completely understanding everything about the world around them. It makes me wonder just how old Puppy actually is. If clowns are born as adults and learn so quickly, it's possible Puppy is as young as five years old. I'm afraid to ask her. I always thought she was my age. But since life is so fast and so short in her world, it's very possible that she's a fraction of my age. It might be possible that clowns rarely live for over a decade.

On weekends, Puppy invites all the children into the house for movie night. She doesn't let them in normally, protective of her own space. Despite caring about her young more than anything in the world, she doesn't want to share her luxuries with them. She doesn't want them impeding on her territory. I'm happy that the interior of our house is not overrun by clowns like the rest of our property, but I can't help but feel guilty. As a parent, I feel like we should provide for them. We should give them more than we give ourselves. But in the dimension of death, clowns put their own survival first. They try to help their children along the way, show them a path to thrive, but they'll ditch their kids in a second if it gets in the way of their own life. I'm not sure how I feel about that way of parenting, but I guess it makes sense in a world where the survival of the species matters more than anything.

Although I'm surrounded by clowns day in and day out, I feel like my phobia has mostly been put at ease. Because these clowns are my wife and children, they don't seem so scary and alien. My children love me. They look up to me and want to spend as much time around me as possible. Although they giggle like lunatics for no reason whatsoever, they don't do anything that creeps me out. They are nothing like the clowns I was afraid of when I was a child.

I'm able to have a good life with Puppy, despite the

oddness of having children in large batches. We have plenty of alone time together and I'm full of happiness whenever I see her smile. But I feel like something is missing in our relationship. I'm not sure what it is. We have fun together, we have a great sex life, we have twenty-three wonderful children and more on the way. But something feels unsatisfying about it all. That's when I realize Puppy is the problem. She used to be passionate about becoming an actress but she put her career on hold to have children. She's allowed her instincts to procreate to take over and forgotten about all her hopes and dreams. I feel bad that she's had to put her life on hold, while I have excelled in my career.

I decide to approach the topic with her. I ask, "Have you thought about getting into acting again? I heard there are some auditions at the local theater. It probably doesn't pay but it would be good to try."

Puppy's eyes light up. "Oh, wow. That would be great. I would love to be in a play someday."

I put my hand on her leg. "So do you think you'll try out?"

She thinks about it for a minute, then her eyes turn from purple to pink. She says, "I don't know. I'm still pregnant. They probably won't want a pregnant woman."

I say, "Well, what about after you give birth? You're due soon."

She shakes her head. "I'll surely get pregnant again right after that. I don't think anyone is casting pregnant clowns right now."

"But you don't have to get pregnant again. We have

plenty of children. We don't need more."

For some reason, my words bug her. "But I want more kids. I want to keep having kids with you for as long as we can."

I don't know how to respond to that. Even after how many we've given birth to, let alone all of the ferals who have been running around the neighborhood, I don't understand why she would think we haven't had enough.

"Are you sure you want to give up on being an actress?" I ask. "I think you would be great. You shouldn't give up on your dreams."

She shakes her head. "I'm not giving up. But I'm a mom now. Having children is the most important thing to me."

I try to argue further, but she won't listen. She hates the idea that she's giving up on her dreams and doesn't want to admit it. Her instincts are telling her to breed as much as possible and she's unable to escape the urge. She doesn't know how to reorganize her priorities so that her own ambitions come first. Maybe if I wasn't pulling in enough money for us, she would try harder. But since she can live happily and spend all of her time making new children, she doesn't seem disappointed in the arrangement. As long as I can provide, she'll never leave the path she's on.

I call my mom for the first time since I married Puppy. It's been a long time. We've texted back and forth regularly, but I haven't mentioned what's going on in my life. I just listen to all of her problems with my dad and stuff she's going through with her annoying neighbors and the repairs she has to do on her house. It's been quite a while since we've spoken in person.

"Are you coming home for Christmas this year?" she asks, the first question out of her mouth.

"Maybe," I tell her. "But if I do I won't come by myself."

My mom is confused. "What do you mean?"

I say, "I'm sorry for not telling you yet, but a lot has been going on in my life lately."

"Didn't tell me what?" she asks.

"I got married last year," I tell her.

She burst into laughter. "Bullshit!"

"I'm serious."

"There's no way you got married," she says.

"I did," I tell her. "We eloped."

Once my mother starts to believe me, she gets upset. Her tone changes from joyful to irritated. "Are you kidding me? You better not have gotten married without telling me about it."

"I'm sorry," I tell her. "I didn't want to make a big deal about it."

"What the hell is wrong with you?" she exclaims. "Why didn't you have a wedding? You're my only child.

Don't you know how important that would have been for me?"

I take a deep breath and explain myself. "I'm sorry, Mom. I was worried about what you'd think about my wife. I didn't want you to object."

"Why would I object?" she asks, infuriated with me. "I wouldn't care who married you. Is she a cam girl or something? I only care that she treats you well."

"She's a clown," I tell her. "She came from dimension 162."

When I say this, my mom's voice goes quiet. I can hear her breaths becoming rapid.

"Don't fucking joke about that," she says.

I'm surprised by her response. I say, "I'm not joking. Her name is Puppy. She's the love of my life."

"But you hate clowns!" she cries. "You've always hated clowns!"

I can't believe my mom is reacting this way. Of all people, I thought she would understand. I figured she'd make fun of me for my phobia, but I never thought she would get mad about it.

"I got over my phobia," I tell her. "I saw a therapist who introduced me to a clown girl. She thought if I got to know one I would let go of my prejudice. It worked too well. We ended up getting married soon after we met."

My mother freaks out on me. "But you can't marry a clown! You've always been afraid of them, so I thought I wouldn't have to warn you away."

"Warn me away from what?"

"Clowns are filthy, horrible creatures," my mom says.

"They've been breeding like cockroaches here. Everyone knows to stay away from them."

"They're not cockroaches. I love Puppy. I love our children."

"Children!" my mom cries. "Don't tell me that you had children with that freak."

"Actually, we have twenty-three children," I say. "We should have more coming soon."

"You better be joking."

"I'm serious. Clowns have a lot of kids. I don't really understand it myself, but they breed a lot faster than humans. Puppy says we'll stop once we have a hundred kids or so."

"A hundred? Are you crazy? You need to leave that woman and come home immediately!"

I shake my head, even though she can't see me over the phone. "I'm not leaving my wife and children. I love them."

"You don't understand," my mom says. "The clowns are everywhere. They're filling our streets, living in tent villages. They killed my neighbor's kid and ate her cats. The clowns are not human. They're evil. Surely you know this, don't you? You're not safe. You have to get out of there as soon as you can."

Her words piss me off. I can't contain myself. I say, "Look, Mom. I'm the happiest I've been in years. I'm not abandoning everything that matters most to me. I love my wife. I love my kids. I don't care that they're clowns. I want to be with them for the rest of my life."

My mom panics at my words. "You're brainwashed.

You have to realize that. Clowns do that to people. They make you think that you're safe with them, but they don't really care about you. Haven't you been watching the news? That clown woman just wants you to give her babies and then she'll kill you once she doesn't need you anymore."

I nearly lose it on her. "Stop being such a bitch, Mom. You're just mad that I didn't marry a blue-eyed blonde like you. Puppy cares about me, more than anyone I've ever known. There are feral clowns out there doing horrible things, but not all clowns are like that. Many of them are good people. If you met Puppy you'd understand. I wanted to bring her to Christmas this year."

My mom raises her voice. "Don't you dare bring her to my home. You keep that monster away from me."

"She's not a monster!"

"Like hell she isn't!"

"Why don't you want me to be happy?"

"I want you to be safe!" she yells at me. "If you don't get away from her, I'm going to call the cops. I'm going to tell them she's holding you hostage."

"Don't you dare!" I cry.

"I'll do it if that's what it takes."

I take a deep breath and calm myself a little, trying to see things from my mother's perspective. "But you have grandchildren now. Doesn't that mean anything to you?"

This makes her quiet down for a minute. I can hear her beginning to cry on the other line.

When she finally speaks through her sobs, she says, "They aren't *my* grandchildren."

91

Then I hang up on her. I can't handle her rejecting my kids that way. If she's not going to accept my family then I don't want anything to do with her. I thought she would be critical. I thought she would make fun of me. But I never expected she would call my wife and children monsters.

My mom tries calling me back, but I don't answer. There's no way I'll let her get in the way of my happiness.

CHAPTER
SEVEN

The clowns spread across the country and then across the globe. Because they have no natural predators in our world, they breed out of control. The government pronounces them an invasive species. Even though they are sentient life, the authorities start treating them as mere pests. Although they take pity on clowns that have jobs and homes, the ones who contribute to society, they don't feel the same way about the clowns that live in the streets. Feral clowns are being hunted down and executed like vermin.

All of my children that have been living in tents in my front yard are moved to the back. I have some of them live up in the attic. Despite being unfinished, the attic is at least safe. Though Puppy doesn't approve, I allow the oldest five of our children to take over the spare room in my house. I build them bunk beds so they'll all fit. Because they are the oldest of our children, I've grown the closest to them. I don't want to see them hurt. The others stay in the backyard, hiding from the police whenever they patrol the alleyway.

"Why are humans so mean?" Puppy cries to me. "I thought we'd be safe here. I thought my children would thrive."

I don't know what to say to her. I pull her into my arms and try to comfort her. "Human civilization wasn't prepared for your people. We have limited resources. The way clowns breed, our world doesn't know how to adapt. The news says our world's population has grown ten times in just the past couple of years. Clowns outnumber humans nine to one. And the other races from other dimensions outnumber us three to one. Humans are scared because they're losing their world to invaders."

"We don't mean to be invaders..." Puppy cries.

I hold her closer. "I know. It's not your fault. But you'll be safe. They're not targeting domesticated clowns like you. Our children will be okay as long as they don't roam the streets at night."

But my words don't comfort Puppy. She cries and buries her face in my chest. She's terrified of what the humans will do to our family.

Our children start to disappear, one at a time. I can control them during the day, but during clown hour they do what they please. Whenever they go roaming the streets at night, my neighbors call the exterminators and they are hunted down. Only Puppy and our first batch of children are safe. Because they don't leave the house during clown hour, they aren't seen as a threat.

After a few months, the government creates laws for even domesticated clowns. They have to register with the Department of Interdimensional Beings. When I take my family to the government office, they say only my wife and four of my children will be accepted. To become real citizens of the country, I need to get them licenses. I want them all to have citizenship. But I make a huge mistake bringing thirty of my children with me to the office. The authorities force me to choose only four of my kids. The rest will be taken away, most likely to be executed or used as slave labor for overseas sweatshops.

Puppy loses it when she hears this. Her eyes turn yellow and her shark teeth widen at the people who say they will take her children. But I hold her back. I know that if she comes across as a feral clown they'll kill her on the spot. It tears me apart, but I know there's no choice but to choose which of our children will be spared. Puppy refuses to be a part of the decision and I'm sure she will resent me for it forever, but I pick my favorite four children. I choose three girls and one boy, all of them from the first batch of offspring. The remaining male from the first batch, the one who looks the most clown-like of any of my children, the one I'm least connected to, is one of the clowns I give up. Even though he didn't deserve to be seen as less than my other children, I couldn't help but let my prejudice take over. I couldn't help but give the poor boy up.

The Department of Interdimensional Beings takes the rest of my children. Even though many of them are more human than clown, they are still rounded up like vermin and sent away, probably to some kind of execution camp. I hope they aren't going to be killed. Even if they are made slaves in some faraway country, I think it would be preferable to them being killed outright. At least they would have hope. At least I would feel better about myself.

When we get home, Puppy can't hold back her disgust with me. Even though my submissive behavior saved her and four of our children, she doesn't see it that way. She just sees me as a coward who couldn't protect his children. She forgives me after a few weeks, but during that time I feel more ashamed of myself than I've ever felt in my life. I wish I had a better way of taking care of my family. I wish I didn't try to save them through the system and found a place outside of civilization where nobody would have ever found them.

Things don't last this way for long. Once clowns realize their strength in numbers, it isn't long before they overthrow the American government. With clowns in power, they can breed without restraint. They don't have to worry about being killed in the streets by racist humans with guns.

Without anything getting in our way, Puppy goes back to breeding with me. She forgives me for everything I've done and wants me to make up for it by giving her three times as many babies as she had before. After a few more litters, our oldest four leave the nest and go seeking mates of their own. Two of them find human mates in our city and one finds another clown to settle down with. The fourth I never hear from again, but I hope she's doing alright. Our firstborn sometimes comes to see us, but the others are so busy they don't have time to visit their old mom and dad.

Puppy isn't so sad that our oldest children are long gone. She focuses on having so many new kids it doesn't matter to her. Before I know it, our yard is full again. We have fifty-five children who stick around our house. They branch out, taking over the houses next door. I'm not sure if my neighbors abandoned their house or if the clowns took care of them without me knowing, but we now have possession of several homes on my block. Since clowns have more rights than humans, unless they are married to clowns, my family is able to take over any house on the block they want. After eight months, my family completely rules the neighborhood. Fifteen houses and three blocks of territory. All of them ours.

I haven't had contact with other humans in a long time. My company closed down soon after the clown takeover and I've been out of work indefinitely. But we don't have to worry about food. Puppy has been planting seeds from her world, growing vegetables from the dimension of death. The plants are dangerous and look like ferocious reptiles when fully grown, but when harvested properly they are able to feed our whole neighborhood without need of money or grocery stores.

We have our section of the street blocked off, guarded from invaders. But it's not prejudiced humans we have to worry about. It's other clowns. Just as Puppy and I have been breeding clowns out of control, other people have been doing the same. And the clowns from other broods are just as territorial as Puppy is. It won't be long before war breaks out between tribes. It's undiscovered country for both humans and clowns. Neither species understands overpopulation. Clowns have never been in a position where their numbers are a problem. It's usually that their numbers can't keep up with their high levels of death. And humans, even in the most populated areas of the world, have no idea how to adapt to a population growth this rapid. It's new territory for all races involved.

The dead body of a human is found in our backyard one day. It's trapped in webs full of clown eggs, stripped of meat and blood. One of my new children must gotten to it during clown hour. When I get a good look at it, I see something familiar. The dead body looks similar to my mother. I wonder if she tried to travel across country to see me, to try to rescue me from my clown wife. I hope it's not true. I hope she stayed in Colorado and lived a happy life with my father. But if this is her, I can't help but feel shame for her. We live in a different world now. Clowns have taken over. There's no room for prejudice. If she can't find a way to integrate with the clowns then she has no hope for survival.

I choose to believe it's not my mother and just some random human passing through. I don't think it would be healthy to blame my children for my mother's death.

When I look out into the street, I notice the homes on our block are falling into ruin. The clowns don't know how to take care of properties. They don't know plumbing or roofing or appliance repair. With humans going into hiding, we're not going to be able to maintain our houses for very long. It's possible we'll all be living on the streets soon, building circus tents made of spider webs to shelter us from the elements. I'm not excited to leave my home, but I know one day it might become reality. The world is no longer like it was. We need to find new ways to live. Clown ways. Human civilization is becoming outdated and I need to leave it behind.

Over the years, Puppy ages. She becomes older than any clown she's ever known. But clowns don't age the same as humans. She doesn't get wrinkled. She doesn't turn gray and fragile. When clowns get to the age of thirty-five, they start growing. They blow up like balloons. Perhaps not males, but the females do. If a clown woman survives long enough, her body assumes she's found a safe enough place to transform. Puppy becomes a gigantic blob of flesh, so big she can no longer leave our bedroom. She becomes a queen clown. Our children bring her food and make sure she's happy and well-protected. They guard her room with swords made from balloons, giggling with excitement for no particular reason. Only I can enter whenever I want to. The other children can only see her when they bring her food.

When I enter the room with Puppy, I'm terrified by what she's become. Her abdomen is swollen so wide I can't even see the other side of the room. The bed has been crushed to the floor beneath her. The ceiling is warping from the pressure of her massive form. Her breasts are two misshapen blobs that droop to the ground like giant beanbag chairs, oozing thick streams of strawberry milk that puddle beneath her. New colors have grown from her body. Blue and purple swirls cover her flesh. She no longer wears any clothes. Nothing fits her anymore. The only thing she wears is a pink bib around her neck.

She doesn't seem to understand the changes she's gone through and smiles at me just as she always did when she resembled a human.

"We've done so well," Puppy tells me. "We've had so many children and they're flourishing. We've eliminated all predators. We can finally be happy."

But when she glares down at me with her triple chin, her thick limbs drooped to the floor, I find it hard to see her as the same Puppy I fell in love with.

"You're happy, aren't you?" she asks. "Do you love me as much as you always have?"

I find myself nodding my head. Although her new form is a bit repulsive, I can't help but love her. She's the perfect woman for me and I can't see myself with anyone else.

"Give me more babies," Puppy says. "With my new body, I can lay hundreds of eggs. We can have more children than we ever thought possible."

Puppy lifts a layer of fat beneath her, spreading the carpet of blue pubic hair between her legs, showing off a monstrous vagina bigger than I am.

"Come to me," she says.

Her vagina oozes with thick glowing fluid, covered in glitter. Despite her grotesque form, I tear off my clothes and go to her. I don't find this blob of a clown attractive, but my body reacts on its own. It's like I'm under a spell. Chemicals in my brain are urging me forward.

When I arrive at her pelvis, I don't know what to do. I let her take the lead. Her blue vagina opens up, releasing a strong sugary odor like cotton candy. Her purple labia wrap around my body and pull me close to her.

"Oh, yeah…" she says, enjoying the feeling of my body against her.

But I have no idea how to make love to her. She's just too big and grotesque. Her fleshy mass writhes against me, forcing me deeper into her vagina. Puppy is desperate for me to make love to her, but I don't understand how. Her arms wrap around me and push me inside, but I'm not able to mate. I can't get an erection. I don't even know how it will work with our size difference.

"Don't you want me?" Puppy asks, staring down at me with blood-red eyes. "Am I not attractive to you anymore?"

I panic when I hear her words. "Of course I'm still attracted to you."

She smiles and says, "Then show me."

I try to give her pleasure with my hands and my mouth, but I still can't get an erection. I can't have sex with her in the way she wants me to.

When Puppy realizes I'm unable to satisfy her, her eyes turn brown. She looks down at me. "What's wrong? You used to get hard just by the sight of me."

I shake my head. "I don't know."

"Just get hard and fuck me," Puppy cries. "You're my mate. I can't do my job without you."

"I don't think I can," I tell her.

Her eyes turn yellow and she cries out in frustration. She grabs me with her muscled arms and lifts me up to her face.

"What do you mean you don't think you can?" she yells at me.

Her voice deepens, sounding masculine and animalistic. She glares at me with her big yellow eyes, exposing her shark-like teeth.

"I'm getting older," I tell her. "I can't get erections like I used to."

She doesn't like my answer, shaking her head at me. Her blue lips foaming with rage. "You're my mate. It's your job to function correctly."

"I'm sorry," I tell her.

She tries to turn me on. She opens her mouth wide and licks me, her fat enormous tongue slathering across my body, trying to get my penis hard. But nothing happens. In her current form, I'm unable to find her sexually attractive.

"Don't you love me anymore?" she asks, almost ready to cry.

"Of course I love you," I say, but even I don't believe my words. She's become like a monster. She's not even a clown anymore. I really don't know if I love her. I don't know if I even see her as my wife anymore.

Puppy sees through my half-hearted lie and becomes infuriated.

"If you won't mate with me then maybe there's another use for you," she cries.

She unhinges her jaws and lifts me up over her gaping mouth.

"Maybe I'll just eat you," she says. "If you can't satisfy me sexually then maybe you'll satisfy me in another way."

I scream at her, struggling in her grasp. I look down at her rows of shark-like teeth, peering down her massive gaping throat. But she doesn't eat me. She just holds me there, trying to get a rise out of me. As though she thinks that scaring me will be a way to get me erect, as though I need danger to want to have sex with her. But I don't get hard. I just writhe in a panic, fighting against her grasp.

Puppy drops me in frustration. She pushes me away.

"Fine," she says. "I don't need you anymore."

I get to my feet, looking up at her with tears in my eyes. "What do you mean by that?"

She sobs at me, jiggling her bulbous form. "If you don't want to have sex with me, how can I call you my mate?"

"I *do* want to have sex with you," I cry. "I'm just not able to right now."

"You hate me!" Puppy yells. "You don't want to give me babies anymore!"

I go to her and wrap my arms around a large fold of belly. "Of course I do. I'll try harder. I promise I'll give you more babies."

Puppy wipes away her tears. "You promise?"

I nod my head. "I'd do anything for you."

But when we try again, trying to get into the mood, rubbing myself against her marshmallow-white flesh, I still can't get an erection. I still can't make love to her properly.

She shoves me away from her.

"Fuck you, asshole!" she cries. "I thought you loved me. I thought no matter what happened we'd always be together."

"We will always be together!" I cry.

She shakes her blobby head, drool spraying across her cheeks. "You've changed. The man I married would never reject me like this."

"I'm not rejecting you!"

She kicks me farther away from her and says, "Get out of here. Never talk to me again. You're not my husband. I don't want anything to do with you."

Her words send me into a panic. "But Puppy, I love you more than anything. Our relationship means more than sex, doesn't it? Even if we never had sex again I'd still love you. You mean everything to me."

After I say this, Puppy's eyes turn cold. They bore into me with a thick black color, one I've never seen before.

Her voice deepens like that of a monster and she says,

"We're over. I'll find someone else to give me babies."

Before I'm able to argue, she calls in the guards. Three of my children come in and pull me away from my wife. They don't see me as their father anymore. They just see me as some kind of an intruder.

I'm kicked out of my own house and forced onto the streets. I desperately plead with my children to let me back in, let me see my wife again. But they just treat me like a stranger. They say if I don't leave they'll be forced to kill me. Without any other course of action, I leave the neighborhood. I go far away, crying at the top of my lungs.

CHAPTER
EIGHT

After I leave the nest I had been in for several years, I feel my brain clearing. It's like an evil spell has been lifted and I've finally come back to my senses. My fear of clowns comes rushing back to me.

I realize I was never in love with Puppy in the first place. I was terrified of her. But she had control of me. She released some kind of pheromones that numbed my fear and made me fall in love with her. Now I know it was all false. Now I know that I was being controlled to help instigate the clown takeover.

As I explore the streets of my city, I realize the clowns have completely overrun the place. There's not a human in sight. I take shelter in abandoned buildings and raid grocery stores at night. So many of the clowns are feral that they don't know how to open canned goods. There's plenty of food to salvage. All I have to do is avoid the clowns and I'll be able to survive.

During clown hour, the streets become filled with deranged laughing clowns. They flood the area, giggling and screaming, running around with their heads twisted back in weird positions. It's like the dreams I used to have as a child. I'm hiding in an abandoned building with hordes of deranged clowns hunting me like zombies. But for some reason, I'm not as afraid as I was in my dreams. I've been around clowns enough to know how they act. I know what to do to stay out of their way during clown hour.

When I leave the city, I meet up with other human survivors. They are people who used to run conspiracy theory websites, the ones warning people about the dangers of clowns. These people have been surviving for a long time and are not about to let the clowns keep our world. They have plans to destroy the gateway to the dimension of death and I'm more than happy to help them accomplish it.

But when they find out I was breeding with a queen clown, they tell me they want me to help to take her down. They want to kill her and all of my children, because they know queen clowns are the most dangerous clowns of them all. Because they can reproduce at such an accelerated rate, they must be eliminated as soon as possible.

At first, I feel happy to be able to help the survivors. I want them to accept me. I want to help their cause. But I can't get myself to give away the location of my wife. Puppy rejected me, but deep down I think I still love her. I can't let her or my children die at the hands of these people. She might be a monster now, but when I think about who she was when we first met I can't help but want to protect her. I just love the woman she was so much. It doesn't matter that she is a clown. She's still the love of my life. I won't betray her no matter what.

When the human survivors realize I won't give up my wife's location, they stop seeing me as an ally. They strap me to a chair and torture me, trying to get the information out of me.

I'm a weak man. I try to fight against the torture, but I can't hold out for long. I tell them my old address. I tell them how many of my children they will be up against. I feel like a horrible person, but I let them have all the information they want in the end.

When the group of freedom fighters goes off to wage war against my family, they leave me by myself, tied to a chair in the middle of nowhere. I struggle against my bonds, fighting to free myself. Because they didn't leave anyone to watch over me, I'm able to eventually wiggle myself loose.

I grab an AR-15 they left behind and go after them. I don't know if I'll be able to stop them, but as a father, I have to try. I can't allow them to kill my children. I can't allow them to hurt Puppy.

Perhaps there are still clown pheromones clogging my senses or perhaps I'm just running on the protective instincts of a father, but I won't let those humans hurt my family.

Human society took thousands of years to get to

where it is. It took a fraction of that time for races from another world to topple everything we know. But the clowns weren't trying to destroy us. They didn't have malicious intent. They were just acting on an instinct to procreate and survive. They just want what's best for their offspring, just like every other living being on the planet.

And I'm on a warpath, ready to kill people of my own race in order to protect my family. Because my instincts are just as valid as everyone else's. I want my children to survive. I want them to flourish and prosper. I will go back home and fight off the attackers even if my children won't accept me anymore. I will go back to my wife and show her I still love her. I will give her all the babies that she wants, even if I have to use salvaged sexual enhancement pills to become erect around her monstrous form. Because I need her in my life. I need to prove to her that I'm man enough to provide for her. Because my biology tells me this is important. My biology has made me a slave to her nature. And I will kill every single person who gets in my way. Because what I want is more important than what they want. My children are more important than their children. It is what my instincts are screaming at me. And we are all imprisoned, without any hope, clown or human, to our primordial instincts.

BONUS SECTION

This is the part of the book where we would have published an afterword by the author but he insisted on drawing a comic strip instead for reasons we don't quite understand.

Thank you for reading my new book, *Why I Married a Clown Girl from the Dimension of Death.* I hope you liked it!

It's me CM3!

When I first started writing bizarro fiction, I promised myself I would never write a clown book.

Not because I hated clowns or anything, but because they seemed so overdone in the small press. Everyone was writing about them.

So I wrote about mutant sex toys and meat planets instead.

I thought I was way too cool for the evil clown kids.

THE **CM3** COLLECTOR'S LIBRARY

Signed limited edition hardcovers of your
favorite books by Carlton Mellick III.

—SUBSCRIBE TODAY—

www.carltonmellick.com/exclusive-hardcovers

ABOUT THE AUTHOR

Carlton Mellick III is one of the leading authors of the bizarro fiction subgenre. Since 2001, his books have drawn an international cult following, despite the fact that they have been shunned by most libraries and chain bookstores.

He won the Wonderland Book Award for his novel, *Warrior Wolf Women of the Wasteland*, in 2009. His short fiction has appeared in *Vice Magazine, The Year's Best Fantasy and Horror #16, The Magazine of Bizarro Fiction,* and *Zombies: Encounters with the Hungry Dead*, among others. He is also a graduate of Clarion West, where he studied under the likes of Chuck Palahniuk, Connie Willis, and Cory Doctorow.

He lives in Portland, OR, the bizarro fiction mecca.

Visit him online at **www.carltonmellick.com**

QUICKSAND HOUSE

Tick and Polly have never met their parents before. They live in the same house with them, they dream about them every night, they share the same flesh and blood, yet for some reason their parents have never found the time to visit them even once since they were born. Living in a dark corner of their parents' vast crumbling mansion, the children long for the day when they will finally be held in their mother's loving arms for the first time. But that day seems to never come. They worry their parents have long since forgotten about them.

When the machines that provide them with food and water stop functioning, the children are forced to venture out of the nursery to find their parents on their own. But the rest of the house is much larger and stranger than they ever could have imagined. The maze-like hallways are dark and seem to go on forever, deranged creatures lurk in every shadow, and the bodies of long-dead children litter the abandoned storerooms. Every minute out of the nursery is a constant battle for survival. And the deeper into the house they go, the more they must unravel the mysteries surrounding their past and the world they've grown up in, if they ever hope to meet the parents they've always longed to see.

Like a survival horror rendition of *Flowers in the Attic*, Carlton Mellick III's *Quicksand House* is his most gripping and sincere work to date.

HUNGRY BUG

In a world where magic exists, spell-casting has become a serious addiction. It ruins lives, tears families apart, and eats away at the fabric of society. Those who cast too much are taken from our world, never to be heard from again. They are sent to a realm known as Hell's Bottom—a sorcerer ghetto where everyday life is a harsh struggle for survival. Porcelain dolls crawl through the alleys like rats, arcane scientists abduct people from the streets to use in their ungodly experiments, and everyone lives in fear of the aristocratic race of spider people who prey on citizens like vampires.

Told in a series of interconnected stories reminiscent of Frank Miller's *Sin City* and David Lapham's *Stray Bullets*, Carlton Mellick III's *Hungry Bug* is an urban fairy tale that focuses on the real life problems that arise within a fantastic world of magic.

STACKING DOLL

Benjamin never thought he'd ever fall in love with anyone, let alone a Matryoshkan, but from the moment he met Ynaria he knew she was the only one for him. Although relationships between humans and Matryoshkans are practically unheard of, the two are determined to get married despite objections from their friends and family. After meeting Ynaria's strict conservative parents, it becomes clear to Benjamin that the only way they will approve of their union is if they undergo The Trial—a matryoshkan wedding tradition where couples lock themselves in a house for several days in order to introduce each other to all of the people living inside of them.

SNUGGLE CLUB

After the death of his wife, Ray Parker decides to get involved with the local "cuddle party" community in order to once again feel the closeness of another human being. Although he's sure it will be a strange and awkward experience, he's determined to give anything a try if it will help him overcome his crippling loneliness. But he has no idea just how unsettling of an experience it will be until it's far too late to escape.

MOUSE TRAP

It's the last school trip young Emily will ever get to go on. Not because it's the end of the school year, but because the world is coming to an end. Teachers, parents, and other students have been slowly dying off over the past several months, killed in mysterious traps that have been appearing across the countryside. Nobody knows where the traps come from or who put them there, but they seem to be designed to exterminate the entirety of the human race.

Emily thought it was going to be an ordinary trip to the local amusement park, but what was supposed to be a normal afternoon of bumper cars and roller coasters has turned into a fight for survival after their teacher is horrifically killed in front of them, leaving the small children to fend for themselves in a life or death game of mouse and mouse trap.

NEVERDAY

Karl Lybeck has been repeating the same day over and over again, in a constant loop, for what feels like a thousand years. He thought he was the only person trapped in this eternal hell until he meets a young woman named January who is trapped in the same loop that Karl's been stuck within for so many centuries. But it turns out that Karl and January aren't alone. In fact, the majority of the population has been repeating the same day just as they have been. And society has mutated into something completely different from the world they once knew.

THE BOY WITH THE CHAINSAW HEART

Mark Knight awakens in the afterlife and discovers that he's been drafted into Hell's army, forced to fight against the hordes of murderous angels attacking from the North. He finds himself to be both the pilot and the fuel of a demonic war machine known as Lynx, a living demon woman with the ability to mutate into a weaponized battle suit that reflects the unique destructive force of a man's soul.

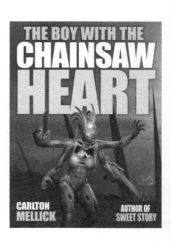

PARASITE MILK

Irving Rice has just arrived on the planet Kynaria to film an episode of the popular Travel Channel television series *Bizarre Foods with Andrew Zimmern: Intergalactic Edition*. Having never left his home state, let alone his home planet, Irving is hit with a severe case of culture shock. He's not prepared for Kynaria's mushroom cities, fungus-like citizens, or the giant insect wildlife. He's also not prepared for the consequences after he spends the night with a beautiful nymph-like alien woman who infects Irving with dangerous sexually-transmitted parasites that turn his otherworldly business trip into an agonizing fight for survival.

In the center of the city once known as Portland, Oregon, there lies a mountain of flesh. Hundreds of thousands of tons of rotting flesh. It has filled the city with disease and dead-lizard stench, contaminated the water supply with its greasy putrid fluids, clogged the air with toxic gasses so thick that you can't leave your house without the aid of a gas mask. And no one really knows quite what to do about it. A thousand-man demolition crew has been trying to clear it out one piece at a time, but after three months of work they've barely made a dent. And then there's the junkies who have started burrowing into the monster's guts, searching for a drug produced by its fire glands, setting back the excavation even longer.

It seems like the corpse will never go away. And with the quarantine still in place, we're not even allowed to leave. We're stuck in this disgusting rotten hell forever.

THE TERRIBLE THING THAT HAPPENS

There is a grocery store. The last grocery store in the world. It stands alone in the middle of a vast wasteland that was once our world. The open sign is still illuminated, brightening the black landscape. It can be seen from miles away, even through the poisonous red ash. Every night at the exact same time, the store comes alive. It becomes exactly as it was before the world ended. Its shelves are replenished with fresh food and water. Ghostly shoppers walk the aisles. The scent of freshly baked breads can be smelled from the rust-caked parking lot. For generations, a small community of survivors, hideously mutated from the toxic atmosphere, have survived by collecting goods from the store. But it is not an easy task. Decades ago, before the world was destroyed, there was a terrible thing that happened in this place. A group of armed men in brown paper masks descended on the shopping center, massacring everyone in sight. This horrible event reoccurs every night, in the exact same manner. And the only way the wastelanders can gather enough food for their survival is to traverse the killing spree, memorize the patterns, and pray they can escape the bloodbath in tact.

BIO MELT

Nobody goes into the Wire District anymore. The place is an industrial wasteland of poisonous gas clouds and lakes of toxic sludge. The machines are still running, the drone-operated factories are still spewing biochemical fumes over the city, but the place has lain abandoned for decades.

When the area becomes flooded by a mysterious black ooze, six strangers find themselves trapped in the Wire District with no chance of escape or rescue.

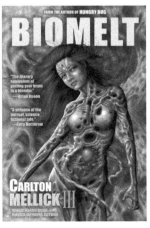

EVER TIME WE MEET AT THE DAIRY QUEEN, YOUR WHOLE FUCKING FACE EXPLODES

Ethan is in love with the weird girl in school. The one with the twitchy eyes and spiders in her hair. The one who can't sit still for even a minute and speaks in an odd squeaky voice. The one they call Spiderweb.

Although she scares all the other kids in school, Ethan thinks Spiderweb is the cutest, sweetest, most perfect girl in the world. But there's a problem. Whenever they go on a date at the Dairy Queen, her whole fucking face explodes.

EXERCISE BIKE

There is something wrong with Tori Manetti's new exercise bike. It is made from flesh and bone. It eats and breathes and poops. It was once a billionaire named Darren Oscarson who underwent years of cosmetic surgery to be transformed into a human exercise bike so that he could live out his deepest sexual fantasy. Now Tori is forced to ride him, use him as a normal piece of exercise equipment, no matter how grotesque his appearance.

SPIDER BUNNY

Only Petey remembers the Fruit Fun cereal commercials of the 1980s. He remembers how warped and disturbing they were. He remembers the lumpy-shaped cartoon children sitting around a breakfast table, eating puffy pink cereal brought to them by the distortedly animated mascot, Berry Bunny. The characters were creepier than the Sesame Street Humpty Dumpty, freakier than Mr. Noseybonk from the old BBC show Jigsaw. They used to give him nightmares as a child. Nightmares where Berry Bunny would reach out of the television and grab him, pulling him into her cereal bowl to be eaten by the demented cartoon children.

When Petey brings up Fruit Fun to his friends, none of them have any idea what he's talking about. They've never heard of the cereal or seen the commercials before. And they're not the only ones. Nobody has ever heard of it. There's not even any information about Fruit Fun on google or wikipedia. At first, Petey thinks he's going crazy. He wonders if all of those commercials were real or just false memories. But then he starts seeing them again. Berry Bunny appears on his television, promoting Fruit Fun cereal in her squeaky unsettling voice. And the next thing Petey knows, he and his friends are sucked into the cereal commercial and forced to survive in a surreal world populated by cartoon characters made flesh.

SWEET STORY

Sally is an odd little girl. It's not because she dresses as if she's from the Edwardian era or spends most of her time playing with creepy talking dolls. It's because she chases rainbows as if they were butterflies. She believes that if she finds the end of the rainbow then magical things will happen to her--leprechauns will shower her with gold and fairies will grant her every wish. But when she actually does find the end of a rainbow one day, and is given the opportunity to wish for whatever she wants, Sally asks for something that she believes will bring joy to children all over the world. She wishes that it would rain candy forever. She had no idea that her innocent wish would lead to the extinction of all life on earth.

TUMOR FRUIT

Eight desperate castaways find themselves stranded on a mysterious deserted island. They are surrounded by poisonous blue plants and an ocean made of acid. Ravenous creatures lurk in the toxic jungle. The ghostly sound of crying babies can be heard on the wind.

Once they realize the rescue ships aren't coming, the eight castaways must band together in order to survive in this inhospitable environment. But survival might not be possible. The air they breathe is lethal, there is no shelter from the elements, and the only food they have to consume is the colorful squid-shaped tumors that grow from a mentally disturbed woman's body.

AS SHE STABBED ME GENTLY IN THE FACE

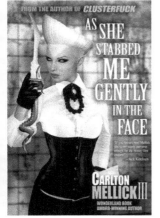

Oksana Maslovskiy is an award-winning artist, an internationally adored fashion model, and one of the most infamous serial killers this country has ever known. She enjoys murdering pretty young men with a nine-inch blade, cutting them open and admiring their delicate insides. It's the only way she knows how to be intimate with another human being. But one day she meets a victim who cannot be killed. His name is Gabriel—a mysterious immortal being with a deep desire to save Oksana's soul. He makes her a deal: if she promises to never kill another person again, he'll become her eternal murder victim.

What at first seems like the perfect relationship for Oksana quickly devolves into a living nightmare when she discovers that Gabriel enjoys being killed by her just a little too much. He turns out to be obsessive, possessive, and paranoid that she might be murdering other men behind his back. And because he is unkillable, it's not going to be easy for Oksana to get rid of him.

CUDDLY HOLOCAUST

Teddy bears, dollies, and little green soldiers—they've all h
enough of you. They're sick of being treated like playthings
spoiled little brats. They have no rights, no property, no hope
a future of any kind. You've left them with no other option-
order to be free, they must exterminate the human race.

Julie is a human girl undergoing reconstructive surgery in or
to become a stuffed animal. Her plan: to infiltrate enemy lin
in order to save her family from the toy death camps. B
when an army of plushy soldiers invade the undergrou
bunker where she has taken refuge, Julie will be forced
move forward with her plan despite her transformati
being not entirely complete.

ARMADILLO FISTS

A weird-as-hell gangster story set in a world where people drive
giant mechanical dinosaurs instead of cars.

Her name is Psycho June Howard, aka Armadillo Fists, a
woman who replaced both of her hands with living armadillos.
She was once the most bloodthirsty fighter in the world of
illegal underground boxing. But now she is on the run from a
group of psychotic gangsters who believe she's responsible for
the death of their boss. With the help of a stegosaurus driver
named Mr. Fast Awesome—who thinks he is God's gift to
women even though he doesn't have any arms or legs--June
must do whatever it takes to escape her pursuers, even if she
has to kill each and every one of them in the process.

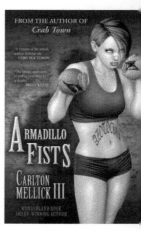

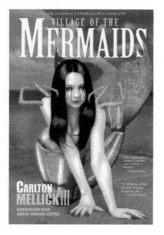

VILLAGE OF THE MERMAIDS

Mermaids are protected by the government under the Enda
gered Species Act, which means you aren't able to kill them ev
in self-defense. This is especially problematic if you happen
live in the isolated fishing village of Siren Cove, where there
ists a healthy population of mermaids in the surrounding wat
that view you as the main source of protein in their diet.

The only thing keeping these ravenous sea women at b
is the equally-dangerous supply of human livestock known
Food People. Normally, these "feeder humans" are enough
keep the mermaid population happy and well-fed. But in Sir
Cove, the mermaids are avoiding the human livestock and ha
returned to hunting the frightened local fishermen. It is up
Doctor Black, an eccentric representative of the Food Peop
Corporation, to investigate the matter and hopefully find a w
to correct the mermaids' new eating patterns before the remai
ing villagers end up as fish food. But the more he digs, the mo
he discovers there are far stranger and more dangerous thin
than mermaids hidden in this ancient village by the sea.

I KNOCKED UP SATAN'S DAUGHTER

Jonathan Vandervoo lives a carefree life in a house made of legos, spending his days building lego sculptures and his nights getting drunk with his only friend—an alcoholic sumo wrestler named Shoji. It's a pleasant life with no responsibility, until the day he meets Lici. She's a soul-sucking demon from hell with red skin, glowing eyes, a forked tongue, and pointy red devil horns... and she claims to be nine months pregnant with Jonathan's baby.

Now Jonathan must do the right thing and marry the succubus or else her demonic family is going to rip his heart out through his ribcage and force him to endure the worst torture hell has to offer for the rest of eternity. But can Jonathan really love a fire-breathing, frog-eating, cold-blooded demoness? Or would eternal damnation be preferable? Either way, the big day is approaching. And once Jonathan's conservative Christian family learns their son is about to marry a spawn of Satan, it's going to be all-out war between demons and humans, with Jonathan and his hell-born bride caught in the middle.

KILL BALL

In a city where everyone lives inside of plastic bubbles, there is no such thing as intimacy. A husband can no longer kiss his wife. A mother can no longer hug her children. To do this would mean instant death. Ever since the disease swept across the globe, we have become isolated within our own personal plastic prison cells, rolling aimlessly through rubber streets in what are essentially man-sized hamster balls.

Colin Hinchcliff longs for the touch of another human being. He can't handle the loneliness, the confinement, and he's horribly claustrophobic. The only thing keeping him going is his unrequited love for an exotic dancer named Siren, a woman who has never seen his face, doesn't even know his name. But when The Kill Ball, a serial slasher in a black leather sphere, begins targeting women at Siren's club, Colin decides he has to do whatever it takes in order to protect her... even if

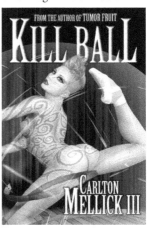

he has to break out of his bubble and risk everything to do it.

THE TICK PEOPLE

They call it Gloom Town, but that isn't its real name. It is a sad city, the saddest of cities, a place so utterly depressing that even their ales are brewed with the most sorrow-filled tears. They built it on the back of a colossal mountain-sized animal, where its woeful citizens live like human fleas within the hairy, pulsing landscape. And those tasked with keeping the city in a state of constant melancholy are the Stressmen-a team of professional sadness-makers who are perpetually striving to invent new ways of causing absolute misery.

But for the Stressman known as Fernando Mendez, creating grief hasn't been so easy as of late. His ideas aren't effective anymore. His treatments are more likely to induce happiness than sadness. And if he wants to get back in the game, he's going to have to relearn the true meaning of despair.

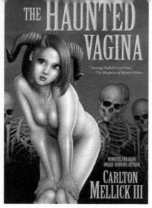

It's difficult to love a woman whose vagina is a gateway to the world of the dead...

Steve is madly in love with his eccentric girlfriend, Stacy. Unfortunately, their sex life has been suffering as of late, because Steve is worried about the odd noises that have been coming from Stacy's pubic region. She says that her vagina is haunted. She doesn't think it's that big of a deal. Steve, on the other hand, completely disagrees.

When a living corpse climbs out of her during an awkward night of sex, Stacy learns that her vagina is actually a doorway to another world. She persuades Steve to climb inside of her to explore this strange new place. But once inside, Steve finds it difficult to return... especially once he meets an oddly attractive woman named Fig, who lives within the lonely haunted world between Stacy's legs.

THE CANNIBALS OF CANDYLAND

There exists a race of cannibals who are made out of candy. They live in an underground world filled with lollipop forests and gumdrop goblins. During the day, while you are away at work, they come above ground and prowl our streets for food. Their prey: your children. They lure young boys and girls to them with their sweet scent and bright colorful candy coating, then rip them apart with razor sharp teeth and claws.

When he was a child, Franklin Pierce witnessed the death of his siblings at the hands of a candy woman with pink cotton candy hair. Since that day, the candy people have become his obsession. He has spent his entire life trying to prove that they exist. And after discovering the entrance to the underground world of the candy people, Franklin finds himself venturing into their sugary domain. His mission: capture one of them and bring it back, dead or alive.

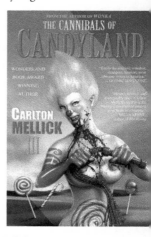

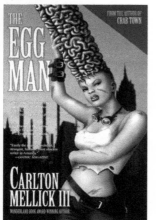

THE EGG MAN

It is a survival of the fittest world where humans reproduce like insects, children are the property of corporations, and having a ten-foot tall brain is a grotesque sexual fetish.

Lincoln has just been released into the world by the Georges Organization, a corporation that raises creative types. A Smell, he has little prospect of succeeding as a visual artist. But after he moves into the Henry Building, he meets Luci, the weird and grimy girl who lives across the hall. She is a Sight. She is also the most disgusting woman Lincoln has ever met. Little does he know, she will soon become his muse.

Now Luci's boyfriend is threatening to kill Lincoln, two rival corporations are preparing for war, and Luci is dragging him along to discover the truth about the mysterious egg man who lives next door. Only the strongest will survive in this tale of individuality, love, and mutilation.

Apeshit is Mellick's love letter to the great and terrible B-horror movie genre. Six trendy teenagers (three cheerleaders and three football players) go to an isolated cabin in the mountains for a weekend of drinking, partying, and crazy sex, only to find themselves in the middle of a life and death struggle against a horribly mutated psychotic freak that just won't stay dead. Mellick parodies this horror cliché and twists it into something deeper and stranger. It is the literary equivalent of a grindhouse film. It is a splatter punk's wet dream. It is perhaps one of the most fucked up books ever written.

If you are a fan of Takashi Miike, Evil Dead, early Peter Jackson, or Eurotrash horror, then you must read this book.

CLUSTERFUCK

A bunch of douchebag frat boys get trapped in a cave with subterranean cannibal mutants and try to survive not by using their wits but by following the bro code...

From master of bizarro fiction Carlton Mellick III, author of the international cult hits Satan Burger and Adolf in Wonderland, comes a violent and hilarious B movie in book form. Set in the same woods as Mellick's splatterpunk satire Apeshit, Clusterfuck follows Trent Chesterton, alpha bro, who has come up with what he thinks is a flawless plan to get laid. He invites three hot chicks and his three best bros on a weekend of extreme cave diving in a remote area known as Turtle Mountain, hoping to impress the ladies with his expert caving skills.

But things don't quite go as Trent planned. For starters, only one of the three chicks turns out to be remotely hot and she has no interest in him for some inexplicable reason. Then he ends up looking like a total dumbass when everyone learns he's never actually gone caving in his entire life. And to top it all off, he's the one to get blamed once they find themselves lost and trapped deep underground with no way to turn back and no possible chance of rescue. What's a bro to do? Sure he could win some points if he actually tried to save the ladies from the family of unkillable subterranean cannibal mutants hunting them for their flesh, but fuck that. No slam piece is worth that amount of effort. He'd much rather just use them as bait so that he can save himself.

THE BABY JESUS BUTT PLUG

Step into a dark and absurd world where human beings are slaves to corporations, people are photocopied instead of born, and the baby jesus is a very popular anal probe.

Milton Keynes UK
Ingram Content Group UK Ltd.
UKHW041817211123
432980UK00001BB/3